My Life in Heavy Metal

My Life in

STORIES BY STEVE ALMOND

Grove Press ☥ New York

Published simultaneously in Canada
Printed in the United States of America

FIRST EDITION

The stories in this book have appeared in the following places: "My Life in Heavy Metal" and "How to Love a Republican," *Playboy;* "Among the Ik," *Zoetrope: All-Story;* "Geek Player, Love Slayer," *Missouri Review;* "The Last Single Days of Don Viktor Potapenko," *Another Chicago Magazine;* "Run Away, My Pale Love," *Ploughshares;* "The Law of Sugar," *The Denver Quarterly;* "The Pass," *New England Review;* "Moscow," *North American Review;* "Valentino," *Other Voices;* "Pornography," *Boulevard;* and "The Body in Extremis" in the anthology *The Ex-Files.*

Library of Congress Cataloging-in-Publication Data
Almond, Steve.
   My life in heavy metal : stories / Steve Almond.
      p. cm.
   ISBN 0-8021-1630-2
   1. Man-woman relationships—Fiction.   I. Title.
PS3601.L58 M9 2002
813'.6—dc21   2001055638

DESIGN BY LAURA HAMMOND HOUGH

Grove Press
841 Broadway
New York, NY 10003

02 03 04 05   10 9 8 7 6 5 4 3 2 1

To my grandparents—
Irving and Anne Rosenthal
and Dorothea and Gabriel Almond
—whose sacrifices have allowed me the luxury of art.

Contents

I slept but my heart was awake.
Listen! My lover is knocking.
—THE SONG OF SONGS

My Life in Heavy Metal

Josephine Byron chased me all through college. Nobody could figure this out, not her friends, not mine, nor the frat boys who watched her wag across the wide lawns of our school. She was one of those women invariably referred to as *striking*, a great big get-a-load-of-that: gleaming black hair, curves like a tulip. Snow White refigured, made warmer, more voluptuous. She was also utterly convinced of herself, her good taste in clothing and men, her beauty and intellect, which she unfurled in earnest, vaguely Marxist jeremiads, while the rest of us gazed at her lips.

In the dim, yeasty haze of after parties and the stoned vistas of Hope Hill, on the cruddy avenues of our college town, Jo came to me bearing gifts, a fresh-baked loaf of bread, a Mardi Gras necklace, bearing her sly smile and plump white breasts. She let me have my way with her, though I was never quite sure, in the end, she wasn't having her way with me. At night, she kissed my body all over and in the mornings made me omelets. It was like having "Happy Birthday" sung to me each day: ecstatic and deeply disquieting.

A few months after graduating I moved to El Paso, where the daily paper needed a clerk. I lived alone, in a basement, and ate fried chicken from boxes. The shower in my place was like being spit on, so I got in the habit of showering at the YMCA, where I swam a few times a week. The lifeguard was a quiet woman who wore clunky glasses and a red Speedo one-piece with a towel wrapped around her lower body. If I stuck around long enough on Wednesdays, she took off the towel and led kiddie classes in the shallow end. She was good with the kids, teasing them in Spanish, holding their bellies while they flailed. Her face was round, bookish, somewhat drab. Even without the glasses her eyes seemed far away. But she cut the water like a nymph.

I spent hours at the paper, hoping to distinguish myself. I sent Jo long, maudlin letters. I wanted her to love me again. I had been wrong to treat her with such disregard. At dusk, when the sun relented, I wandered El Paso's ragged downtown, wallowing in a sadness I considered sophisticated and insoluble. The plaza was always emptying: *vendedores* and day maids trudging back to Juárez, the sweet stale scent of lard punching out from El Segundo Barrio, the thrum of swamp coolers fallen away. Later, the smelting plant would fire up its chimneys and smoke would drift over the Franklin Mountains, which shadowed the city like a row of brown shrugs. To the east lay the trim, eerie avenues of Fort Bliss. To the west, the terraced estates of Coronado, where the swimming pools glowed like sapphires.

For seven months I handled weddings and obits. Then the pop music critic quit, and the managing editor, lacking other recourse, allowed me to sub. El Paso was, still is, part of the vast spandex-and-umlaut circuit that runs the length of I-10. I reviewed virtually every one of the late-eighties hair bands at least once: Ratt, Poison, Winger, Warrant, Great White, White Snake, Kiss, Vixen, Cinderella,

Queensryche, Skid Row, Def Leppard, Brittney Foxx, and Kiss without makeup. At my first concert, Metallica, the band's new bassist introduced himself to the crowd by farting into his microphone. This was the heavy metal equivalent of a *bon mot*.

Because we were a morning paper, I had to bang out my copy by midnight. I operated on a template involving an initial bad pun, a lengthy playlist—*adjective, adjective, song title*—and a description of the lead singer's hair. The rest was your standard catalog of puking yayas, flung undies, poignant duets with the rhythm guitarist back from rehab. I loved the velocity of the process: an event witnessed and recorded overnight. I loved the pressure, the glib improvisation; I loved seeing my byline the next day, all my pretty words, smelling of ink and newsprint.

And the truth is I loved the shows. I remember standing in the front row as Sebastian Bach, the lead singer of Skid Row, screeched "Youth Gone Wild." Bach was the quintessential metal front man, a blond mane and a pair of cheekbones. He strutted the stage like a drag queen, while the lead guitarist yanked out an interminable solo and the drummer became a shirtless piston. It was formulaic and mercenary and a little pathetic. But when I stared down the row, I saw twenty heads banging in unison, like angry mops. These were kids lousy with the bad hormones of adolescence, humiliated by the poverty of their prospects, and this was their dance, their chance to be part of some larger phallic brotherhood; the notes lashed their rib cages, called out to their beautiful, furious wishes.

I'd spoken to the lifeguard a few times, about holiday hours, lane dividers. I imagined having sex with her constantly. I did the same thing with the newsroom prospects, though with the life-guard it was always more exciting, because we were both almost naked.

Her name was Claudia, pronounced in the beautiful Spanish manner, as three distinct, rolling syllables: *Cloud-i-ahh.* She lived by herself, in an apartment not far from the Y.

Every couple of weeks, I took her to some show or another. The idea was that some spark would leap between us. Then we would sneak into the Y, fuck on the squeaky tile, with her bent over a stack of kickboards, or underwater. But she was impossible to read behind her glasses. Our dates were like the ones I had in tenth grade, the tense drive to the mini-golf place, the exhausting formality, the burps unburped.

She spoke in the manner of a kindergarten teacher, softly, a bit too clearly, though when she took up Spanish her lisp blossomed and the tip of her tongue danced along her teeth. I felt sure this animation was a sign of some secret life behind her reticence.

What were we, exactly? Friends, I suppose. Companions in a certain lonely, postgraduate phase. Markers of time.

Besides, there was Jo, beautiful Jo, who called me every other week-end, who seemed to be remaining, in her final year of college, faith-ful to me, assuredly against the counsel of her friends. And who, true to her word, did appear, just a few weeks after her own gradu-ation, marched up the jetway in red suede boots and nearly tackled me. Everyone just stared.

How nice it was to have a beautiful woman tackle me, to feel the eyes of the world upon me again, to have a long, soapy body over which to kvell. And how romantic I made El Paso seem. The plaza! The dollar movies! The oceanic desert! I took her to the lookout point at the top of the Franklins, where we necked and, amid the high schoolers and clumps of creosote, made the sweet foolish talk of love renewed.

A few days after she'd flown back East, Jo called. "I bought my ticket," she said.

"Your ticket?"

"I'm coming out there. To live."

There was a pause, during which I tried very hard to recall whether we had discussed this plan, while also recognizing that I was expected to make some perfectly spontaneous sound of approval, thanksgiving, hosanna, and, in fact, even as I grasped this, grasped that I had failed, let the moment pass and would now be held accountable, asked to explain, possibly more than once, why I hadn't, didn't I love her, hadn't I wooed her for a year solid, questions which seemed perfectly reasonable but which I felt incapable of answering because my head was full of pudding.

That Sunday I took Claudia to the Metalfest at Bayshore, an artificial lake in the middle of absolutely nowhere, New Mexico. Children tended to drown at Bayshore. No one knew why. The lake was only three feet deep.

Heavy metal is an indoor genre. It requires reverberation, darkness, forced proximity. Without these, the crowd loses the sense of itself as a powerful tribe. The elaborate fantasy world of smoke and tinted lights and catwalks just doesn't work on a stage overlooking scrub.

The headliner, Jon Bon Jovi, seemed to recognize this. He took one gander at the pallid crowd and began casting about for a trap-door. His bangs frizzed in the heat; his tights bunched. His falsetto drifted up and away with the dust. The show felt forced, and, in the way of such things, a little sad.

Afterward, I drove Claudia back to town. "So anyway," I said, "it looks like that friend of mine from college, Jo, is going to be heading out."

Claudia looked down into her lap. "I guess I won't be seeing you as much, then."

"Don't be silly," I said. "Why shouldn't I see you?" We hadn't done anything, after all. We were just . . . whatever we were.

"She'll be living with you?"

"Yeah. That's sort of the plan."

"When's she coming out?"

"Next Sunday," I said.

There was a difficult pause. Claudia stared out the windshield. The tops of her ears looked tender from the sun. "It doesn't seem fair," she said finally. She glanced at me and smiled a little. "You know, you get something, and I lose a friend."

"I don't know why you're saying that," I said. "It's not like that."

Claudia called me at work the next day. She wanted to have dinner on Saturday night.

"Sure," I said. "Where do you want to go?"

She giggled. "Why don't you make me dinner?"

Claudia showed up in a black dress and blue eye shadow. Her voice seemed oddly pitched, a bit too exuberant. She gulped at her wine and let the hem of her dress ride up her legs, which looked polished. I didn't have much to say. Nor did she. We were just waiting around for the alcohol to spring our bodies.

We moved to the couch, where we leaned and leaned and finally fell against one another sloppily. I slid my chin down her belly.

She was so much smaller than Jo, almost delicate, but when her knees slipped behind my head they clamped me so hard my bottom row of teeth bit into the underside of my tongue. I could taste my own blood and this mixed with the slightly acrid taste of her. Gradually, her legs sagged to the bed. Her pelvis vaulted into the air. I followed her up, pressed harder, and suddenly there was a warm liquid coming out of her, a great gout of *something* sheeting across my cheeks, down my chin, splashing onto the comforter. I figured, at first, she had urinated. But there was simply too much fluid coming out of her. By the time Claudia had regained her wits, and lowered herself to the bed, the puddle on my comforter was two feet across.

"Are you okay?" I said.

Claudia nodded bashfully and stumbled to the bathroom.

My second theory was that, as a lifeguard, pool water had somehow accumulated inside her and been released when her internal muscles relaxed. But the liquid was as tasteless and odorless as rain.

And you know what? I was goddamn thrilled. It was such a freakish thing she'd done. Claudia, this quiet little mermaid, with her spectacles and her lisp, with her dull brown eyes, who never so much as touched herself so far as I could tell, had not only surrendered her body to me but expelled, spumed, *ejaculated* some mysterious orgasmic juice all over my face. I felt like doing a victory lap around the puddle.

*   *   *

Jo felt my basement apartment was, as she put it, "the kind of place where a serial killer lives." She needed sun, she explained. And a porch.

Our new place was on the fourth floor of a brick building in Sunset Heights, El Paso's historical district. The neighborhood sat on a small rise overlooking the Rio. Locals once had watched Pancho Villa's forces battle *federales* on the plains below. The view now was of the *colonias*, the sprawling cardboard cities that enveloped Juárez proper.

Our apartment was bright and dusty. Every day a new piece of furniture appeared, or a houseplant. Jo made forays into Juárez, carrying back masks, wall hangings, a black leather whip I hoped to employ in some splendidly incompetent sex game but which was instead suspended tastefully over the divan. The kitchen began to fill with utensils—not just forks and spoons, but garlic presses and salad spinners. With a great, perhaps even vicious, efficiency, Jo erased the vestiges of my bachelordom. Closets became places where clothing was *hung*.

I arrived home one day to find the bed decked out in new colors. Jo wandered in from the other room. "What do you think?"

"Nice," I said. "Very colorful."

"I knew you'd like it." She hugged me. "It's Guatemalan."

I paused. "What happened to my old comforter?"

"Salvation Army."

"You gave it away?"

Jo slipped her hand into one of my back pockets and gave me a playful squeeze. "Don't you like this one? We can give it a test-drive if you're not sure."

"Yeah. No. It's nice. I just don't understand why you needed to throw the old one out."

"I didn't throw it out, David. I gave it to charity. It had a stain."
Jo began unbuttoning my shirt.

"What stain?"

"A huge disgusting stain. Right in the middle."

I felt a fizz in my chest. "Whatever happened to washing?" I murmured.

"If you loved the thing so much," Jo said, "you should have washed it yourself."

Mostly, though, we had this beautiful new life. We went to a lot of parties. We took road trips along the rambling old highways of New Mexico and stopped in obscure towns for pie. We slept in on Sundays.

Sometimes, late afternoon, we would lie in the hammock strung across our balcony and watch thunderheads lip over the Franklins, releasing spindles of lightning. Everything changed when the rains came: the desert turned a rich brown and threw up the mulchy scent of creosote. Boys fluttered like salmon in the flooded gutters below. The slag heaps behind the smelter gave off the dull wet sheen of solder. Over in the *colonias*, mamas filed out of shanties to wash their children and fill metal drums with drinking water and thank the Lord.

Afterwards we listened to the world trickle and waited for the honeyed colors of dusk. With the sky suddenly cleared of smog, we could see all the way to the sierras south of Juárez, which looked like giant bones against the thirsty soil.

I took Jo to see Mötley Crüe. Probably it would have been better to start her off on Poison, one of the ballad bands. She kept looking at the front man, Vince Neil. He wore a suit of studded black leather, elevator shoes, a choker. "He's kidding," Jo shouted. "It's a joke, right?"

Neil leapt onto a speaker. "How many of you guys are gonna get some fucking poooontang tonight?"

The crowd went apeshit. The bass started in, along with the drums; the plastic seats began to quiver. Then a noise like wheels hitting a runway, which meant the guitars, churning down to their appointed chords. Jo looked as if she'd been struck in the back of the head with an eel. I'd given her a pair of earplugs, but the affect of 105 decibels is as much seismic as auditory. Strobe lights popped. Neil howled. His voice was a rapture of violent want, released to the crowd and returned in ululating waves. All around us, skinny boys emptied their bodies of sound. Everything about them banged. *Bang bang bang.* Their hair whipped the air, their slender arms knifed in around us.

I found Jo on the steps outside the arena, head between her knees. "If they could just turn it *down* a little," she said.

"Go ahead and take the car," I said. "I'll catch a ride from the night editor."

I figured Jo would be asleep when I got home. But she was sitting up in bed, a towel wrapped around her head.

"Feeling better?" I said.

"Yeah. How was the rest of the show?"

"No big deal. Nikki Sixx flashed the crowd his weenie, so that was pretty cool."

Jo took a sip of tea and fixed me with one of her concerned looks. "You don't really like that stuff," she said.

I had hoped this might be one of those times where we let our differences be. "You sort of have to get into the spirit of the thing," I said.

"What spirit would that be? The spirit of misogynist inner-ear damage?" She shook her head. "You don't like it. You're just being ironic."

"Okay," I said. "I'm going to go brush my ironic teeth."

"And that singer guy," Jo said. "What a getup. He looked like a piece of bad furniture. What's he supposed to be, some kind of stud? Some kind of big ladies' man?"

"It's a show," I said. "Showmanship."

"What gets me is that kids are paying money to listen to that crap. It's so indulgent. In a place like this, with so much *real* suffering."

"You shouldn't take it so seriously."

Jo waited a beat. "You do," she said. "You spend half your life interviewing these guys and critiquing their shows."

"Reviewing," I said. "It's my job to review them. I'm the reviewer."

"I'm sorry. I know it's your job. But isn't it a little sad?"

"I think you're missing it," I said.

"What am I missing? Is there something really deep going on, David? Please, educate me." Jo pulled the towel off her head and let her hair fall. She was acutely aware of her own props.

"The music helps certain kids sort of get in touch with their feelings."

"Their *feelings*? What, exactly, does *poooontang* have to do with their feelings?"

"The music itself. The physical part." I had, at that time, grown my hair into a rather unfortunate mullet: short in front, long in back. And sometimes, in the dim light of one or another arena, the notebook would fall to my side and the music would surge through me and I would bang softly. "What is it that you want from these kids, exactly? Can't you just let them have their thing?"

Jo looked at me with her big green eyes. "They should grow up. They should learn to have some respect for themselves and quit trafficking in such lousy fantasies."

"Easier said than done," I said.

I took Claudia to see Ted Nugent. She didn't like metal much, either. But she was quieter about her contempt and didn't say a word, even as we arrived back at her place, undressed, and reached through the dark. We knew what we were doing. It was disgusting and terrific. Afterwards, I washed up and slipped my clothes on and felt an odd sense of buoyancy, of floating awkwardly into the authentic and forbidden.

On our six-month anniversary as cohabitants, Jo fixed portobellos in a cream sauce with sautéed shallots. I wanted to check out this new local band, Menudo Anti-Christ. Instead, we were going to see Ray Barratto. That was what Jo liked: Latin jazz. Any kind of jazz. I couldn't understand the stuff. I would sit there and listen and listen and wait for the songs to *begin*.

We were with a bunch of our friends, Jo's friends is what they were, people brimming with statistics and good intentions, people engaged in *projects*, people who used words such as *empowerment* and nodded meaningfully when they talked to you.

Guys kept putting tequilas in front of Jo. They wanted to see her poise on display. She got up to dance and now the whole club watched, the young cats sipping gin and the lonely Corona dykes and Barratto himself, the droopy old *conguero*, long past such uncomplicated pleasures, tittering at the motion of her hips, bidding her this way and that with his thick fingers and his drum.

She wobbled in her red suede boots and laughed and insisted she was fine. Then she and a friend went to the bathroom and only the friend returned. Gallantry now demanded that I enter the ladies' room. That was fine with me. I liked the idea! I imagined a bright alcove full of dishy women putting on lipstick and talking cock. But the place was empty and smelled sort of disappointing. A gurgle came from the far stall. Jo looked as if she'd been dropped from a helicopter. The tile pressed against her cheek. Her legs were bent in a few directions. She smiled the glassy smile of the non-ambulatory. On the drive home she threw up twice more, dainty little strings of puke.

How stunning she looked laid out on our bed—like a beautiful corpse! I pressed a washrag to her forehead.

"I'm dying, David. I'm going to die."

"You're not dying, sweetie."

"I'm gonna fall asleep and throw up and drown on my throw-up. Like that guy from the Doors."

"That was Hendrix," I said delicately.

"I'm going to *die*, David. Tell me you love me." Jo closed her eyes. The lids were round and soft purple. They made her look terribly vulnerable. "Don't lie to me," she said. "I love you, David. Don't lie to me."

"Yes."

"Yes what?"

"Yes, I love you."

"How much?"

"A lot."

"How much lot?"

"Infinity lot," I said. "Infinity to the infinity power lot."

Jo smiled. Her teeth were totally unstoppable. It seemed in-conceivable to me, at that moment, that I would fail her. I could see what she had in mind: the settling down, the having of chil-dren, the long, good promise. Motherhood would make her glow like a planet.

"Gimme kiss," she said.

The tequila was coming off her in yellow fumes I found not undesirable. I began, then, to undress her. She squirmed. Moonlight hung in the window and advanced along her body. The skin over her heart flickered.

"Where are you going?" Jo said.

"Nowhere."

"Don't go."

"I'm just going to take my clothes off."

"Don't. I'll fall asleep. I'll drown."

"I'm right here."

"You can't ever leave me. Kiss. *Mmmmm.* Kiss again."

Claudia couldn't cook. Her specialty was *flautas,* which tasted of burned lard. She said the recipe was from her mother. There was always never much to talk about. Her sister was getting engaged. Ozzy Osbourne was coming to town. We drank wine from green jugs.

Without glasses, Claudia's face looked naked. She blinked a great deal. Her skin smelled faintly of chlorine at all times. Our coupling remained hurried and incompetent. Claudia preferred the lights low. We never, ever spoke. But always, there came a moment when her body unclenched; her eyes lost focus and the torrent began. This was just how she was built, though I was convinced it *meant* something.

The idea I had was to do it in the bathroom. I liked the way her thighs bulged against the white of the sink. I liked the light, which was a little too bright, which fringed our skin in yellow, lent us a crispness I associated with interrogation.

I knew there was a complicated person living inside Claudia's body. A reason she wasn't living at home, a reason she was involved with me. She had her own hopes stashed somewhere. But I wasn't interested in those. I wanted only an accomplice.

I reached down and Claudia threw her legs a little wider. Her mouth went sloppy. Her eyes half closed. Water began gushing down the soft skin of her thighs. I pressed forward, and the water, wanting out, pressed back. The sensation was warm and almost painful. Then I felt myself begin, and pushed in all the way. Claudia shrieked. Her head thumped the mirror. There was a sharp crack, a rapid downward motion, and water. Geysers of water, gurgling up, sweeping down. We lay tangled on the floor. I could see blood threading the puddle near my head. Claudia, I was certain, had exploded. Then I saw the sink, toppled nearby. The leads to the water pipes had snapped clean off.

Jo met me at the door. This was maybe one in the morning. I was pretty well sobered up by then.

"What the hell happened to you?" she said.

"In what sense?"

"In the sense that you left the paper four hours ago, and your hair is wet."

"Claudia's fucking toilet overflowed," I said. "I had to take a shower."

Jo stood directly in front of me. She didn't say anything. I could see the blood in her cheeks spiraling.

"It was disgusting." I said. "Believe me. You should be glad I took a shower."

"I want to know what the hell's going on with that woman, David."

"Claudia? What's going on with Claudia? I would guess she's mopping right about now."

"If you're fucking lying to me, David. If you're fucking that woman—"

"Hold on," I said. "Just slow down—"

"Look at me, David."

"I am looking at you. I'm looking right at you." I could feel an awful, thrilling current inside me. "Now you listen to me," I said. "If I were fooling around, if I were flouncing off to fuck this woman, don't you think, did it ever occur to you, that I might be a little more *subtle* about it? That I wouldn't try to do it right under your nose?"

Jo took a half step back. "Why can't I meet her, then?"

"You can," I said. "You can meet her any time you want. I've told you. Do you want to call her right now, and have her come over and you can ask her if I fuck her and then come back here and sleep with you? Is that what you want?" I was breathing through my nose now. My chest was puffed up like a gamecock. "Because you obviously don't believe me. You don't believe I could just be friends with this woman."

"I didn't say I didn't believe you."

"You might as well have." Behind her rose El Paso's new civic center, which was supposed to be a sombrero but looked more like a flat tire. Farther out, the barrel fires of the *colonias* danced like matchsticks. "Look," I said. "Claudia was part of my life before you came here. Maybe that's why I hold her apart a little. The truth is she's a pretty unhappy person. Troubled. And a part of me feels like she needs my company. She's not like you, honey. She doesn't have the world at her feet."

"Who says I have the world at my feet?" Jo said quietly.

I grazed my fingers along her cheek. "You can't keep doing this to yourself. You've got to trust me, baby."

Was it wrong for me to want to protect Jo from such terrible hurt? From a part of myself she was better not knowing? Was it wrong to preserve her belief in me? After all, I wanted to believe just as much as she did—in my own decency, in our bright future together. I wanted to make her happy. This other business, as I saw it, was just something I needed to work out of my system. It would never have occurred to me back then that behind all my fancy footwork was a darker sin: I didn't love Jo as she loved me. I knew only that I felt guilty all the time, unworthy and resentful and complicated. And so, every few weeks, I went out and drowned myself in loud song and copulation and this made me feel simple. And when I returned home, I told Jo heroic lies that defended us both from the ruinous truth.

I didn't love her as she loved me. What other sin is there, finally?

Jo was on the phone in the other room. "Oh my God!" she cried out. "That's so amazing!" A couple of minutes later, she came in the bedroom, puffy and exorbitant.

"That was Kirsten."

"Who?"

"*Kirsten.* My best friend from high school. She's getting *married.* She wants me to be a *bridesmaid.*"

I nodded at the closet, where her other gowns hung. "Peach chiffon or teal?"

"Very funny," she said.

"When's the big day?"

"November twentieth."

"Not *this* November twentieth?" I screwed on a tight little smile.

"Don't you dare," Jo said. "Don't you dare pull this shit. I am not going to this wedding alone because you have to review some idiotic band."

"Guns N' Roses," I said, "is not just some band."

You have to understand: I had interviewed Kip Winger three times. I knew the names of his pets. I had memorized, without any intention of doing so, the words to "Headed for a Heartbreak." Possibly better than anyone else *on earth* I recognized the depths to which heavy metal had sunk. The intensity and musicianship of its earliest practitioners had given way to pretty-boy schlock. This is what made the Gunners so compelling. They represented a return to the core values of the genre, the angry hedonism, the dramatic release. I doubt Axl Rose would have described himself as an Aristotelian, but that is what he was. His voice ramped forever up, toward catharsis.

I had explained all this to Jo, several times. But she just looked at me like my head was on fire. "What we're talking about, David, the issue, is whether you're coming with me to this wedding."

"I'm not," I said.

"This is Kirsten," she said dramatically. "This is one of my best friends."

The trick with Jo was to let her self-regard run down a little. Then to pause, always to pause, which conveyed thought. And then to assume a softer tone. "I know it's important," I said. "I hear you. But this is important to me, honey. It's my job. And I know you think it's just bullshit, but it's also something I value. Can you understand that?"

We were, all things considered, in a phase of expectant compromise. The paper had nominated me for a three-month stint at *USA Today,* in D.C., where I hoped to earn my wings in the world of depthy glitz. Jo was talking with Nader's people about a job. Marriage wasn't on the table just yet. But—as I now gently reminded her—the end of my metal days was in sight. Couldn't she give me this one last hurrah?

Later, in bed, she made me promise. "I want Washington to be different."

"Of course it'll be different," I said. "It's a whole different city."

"You know what I mean," she said.

She closed her eyes and smiled a little and for a second I could see her at sixty, with a bolt of white hair and skin too tired to shine all the time.

"Who're you going to take?" she said.

"One of the sports guys, probably."

"What about Claudia? I haven't heard about her for a while."

"She's got a new boyfriend," I said. "A cop, I think."

It would be fair to call the show a letdown. Loosed from the studio firmament, Axl's voice came across as chalky and unmodulated, the bark of a hungry seagull. Slash was so drunk he kept falling over. A roadie had to scurry onstage and prop him up again. This grew disheartening.

My review was indignant. The band was taking its fans for granted, squandering a hallowed opportunity, retreating from the mandates of thus and such. I clacked away on my laptop in the empty cavern of the coliseum as, down below, the roadies broke down the lights and drum risers and mikes.

Claudia was where I'd left her, on a bench near the back exit. When I'd told her about the move to D.C., she'd only looked down and nodded. It was what she'd expected all along, I guess. But now, as I approached her, sitting there in her sad little blouse, I wanted to be able to do something for her, some terrific, unassailable thing that might restore the magic she held as a lifeguard (a guarder of lives!), quiet and secretly powerful so long ago.

"Let's grab a drink," I said.

"I should be getting home."

"Nonsense." I took her hand. "We'll have some wine. We'll go to my place and have some wine." And as we moved out into the night, with its sooty breath and slender moon, I understood that Claudia was one of those people who is acted upon; that imposing her own desires invited risks she felt unprepared to take.

When I moved into her for the last time, she closed her eyes and lay back and her smell, chlorine and skin lotion, mingled with Jo's perfume, which rose from the sheets. I was in no hurry. I had dropped Jo off at the airport six hours earlier. She would be landing in New York, combing out her hair, wrestling with the overhead compartment. I gave no thought to the weather back East. El Paso, after all, was sweltering.

Claudia's knees began to tremble. Her toes dug at my calves and her mouth went slack. With each thrust, I could hear the faint clack of her teeth. And when her hips began to tilt up, I reached down to caress her, that her body might open and bring the miracle of water. I had a vision, even then, with all that had happened, was about to happen, that I might bow my head between her legs and be washed.

When you live with someone, you come to recognize the way they move, the pace and gravity of their gait. It's the way of our kind: we can't help but reveal ourselves. Jo always took the stairs two at a time, favoring her right leg from an old ballet injury, executing a little hop-skip on the landings. And now, somehow, despite the fact that she was thousands of miles away, I could hear the dangerous jig of her footsteps drawing closer. Claudia began to moan and her body opened and released the water and I felt my own body reaching ecstatically to repeat itself.

The door slammed. Our bodies slammed. Jo's voice sounded out my name. Claudia grabbed at my face for a kiss. One red suede boot appeared in the doorway. I looked down at the glistening contortion of Claudia's body. I still believed I might have time, that there was so much time left to me, to behave like this. And then Jo stepped into the room and looked at us and the air inside her seemed to crumple.

She began to sob, then to choke on her sobs. Her face turned a deep red. It was clear she could not breathe. Claudia's hips gave way, fell to the sheets with a damp smack. She was facing away from the door, still lost in the innocent spell of pleasure. Then she noticed my face and her head swung around and she saw Jo and began weeping too, a soft sound like neighing. Her legs drew up and curled beneath her. Her painted toes looked like little dabs of blood. There was nothing to say. There was that room and the three bodies inside it. Claudia was hyperventilating. Jo was not breathing.

Or rather, she was attempting to breathe, to draw air into her lungs, but failing. Her body made a hundred silent hiccups; her lips were drawn over her teeth in a grimace. Her eyes were pinched shut. If we'd had a child, a little baby girl, this is how she would have looked at birth, drowning on the air of some cold white room.

I must have made a gesture toward her, because her body recoiled and she backed out of the room, bent at the waist, like a servant who has intruded unforgivably on the master's privacy. I stood at the edge of the bed. A draft from the window moved across my absurd little penis. I felt a soft spearing in my side. Earlier, I'd laid down a towel, meaning to slip it beneath Claudia, and now I drew this around me and went after Jo. I had the idea that I still had something to do with her.

She was in the hall, staggering toward the landing. If I could see her face. I so wanted that—to see her face.

"Breathe," I said. "You've got to breathe, baby." I reached out to touch the scrolls of black hair pasted to her temples. Her throat clicked and her voice, finally catching, produced the thick vibrato of agony. Her hand raked my face.

Then she was flying down the stairs, and I charged after her, yelling *wait wait*, yelling, *Oh God, honey.* The neighbors hung from their doorknobs. On the second floor, I got my hand on her shoulder, tried to sort of tackle her, but she threw me off and I landed on my tailbone. A few seconds later the door below clanged. I struggled to my feet and raced down and bounded outside. My towel had fallen away. I was naked in the street, blood smeared on my cheek.

Someone had called the police, I guess, because a squad car was gliding to a stop in front of our building. The cop squinted at me through his tinted windshield and I ducked back, hid in the shadow of the door, watched Jo sprint into the night and disappear.

Claudia was gone, too. *Poof.* There was only a stain on the bed. I checked the bathroom, the closets, everywhere. And then it occurred to me what had happened: she had jumped out the bedroom window. There would be her body, on the sidewalk, and the police would want to know what it was all about.

But this was only some gaudy male fantasy. There was nobody down below but the cop, standing outside his squad car. He looked mean and confused. His hand rested absently on the butt of his gun. And somewhere farther off in the desert, a radio was playing, Axl Rose's tiny voice reaching out, singing: *Take me down to the Paradise City where the grass is green and the girls are pretty.*

And now you listen to me, you people with your poise and careful judgments: These are the things I did. And I was punished for them, as we are all punished, in the end, for the degradations we inflict upon those who love us. Sorrow waits, with the patience of a psalm, for the infidel.

Though what returns to me now is how I felt afterwards, on those certain evenings, driving home toward Jo, sweet Jo, still a little drunk, bearded in the smell of Claudia, weaving the empty lanes of I-10, the warehouses sliding past, El Paso's downtown like an isle of dinky lanterns, the Rio flowing black, and beyond, the speckled blue lights of Juárez. How full my heart was of gratitude! *Thank you,* I wanted to call out. *Thank you! Thank you!*

And if, as was often the case, a cassette were playing, the dumb blunt exuberance of the band, the howl and drub of all those fierce desires would gather in the night above me and become one desire and merge with my desire and confirm that I was doing something even noble in the eyes of youth, radical, kickass, seeking love on all fronts, transporting myself beyond the reach of loneliness and failure, into the blessed province of poontang.

It is in these moments of tender and ridiculous nostalgia that I know something inside me is still broken.

Among the Ik

Rodgers was a nervous man and now, with his wife dead, he was even worse. He had a story to tell but kept insisting he was no good at stories. His hands flapped about like loose cardboard. His tremendous nose, which might have made another man feel powerful, bloomed red with agitation.

"This was, oh gosh, this was back in the sixties. Is it that long now? Yes. It must be. We'd just graduated from the University of Chicago and we were looking for work. *I* was looking for work I should say. This was before Connie and I, before we were married. I went to some conference or other and met this nice old fellow and, you know, everyone was looking for work back then. He said I should send my material along, would I do that, and a few months later he called and asked if I would like to teach at Newton College. There was none of this business of search committees, interviews. I was twenty-three years old, maybe twenty-four. A silly age." Rodgers giggled tentatively. He was speaking to a friend of his daughter's, a tall fellow named Ken who had arrived that afternoon in a gale of slightly forced cheer.

They were at the kitchen table, regarding one another over the leavings of dinner: crumpled napkins, bits of risotto stiffening on flatware, a shank bone whose joint shone faintly blue under the track lighting. The table itself was yellow pine, a stern piece of furniture Rodgers had once hoped to extend with leaves and move into the dining room. As he spoke with Ken, he envisioned running his hand across its surface, though the wood had dried and gone splintery in the last few years. That was the problem with yellow pine.

Rodgers's three children were in the living room, sitting around the fire, peeling tangerines and playing with his baby granddaughter. They had descended upon him for the holiday, an intended gesture of support that filled his house with ruckus.

Connie's death had not been sudden. But Rodgers had somehow experienced it as sudden, not quite believing until belief was no longer a choice but a condition. He found, in her absence, that his children frightened him. He drifted about their busy conversations, offering an observation or pun, enough to keep himself from drawing the suspicion of despair.

Ken was a Ph.D. student who knew enough anthropology to pretend at understanding, and they spent dinner chattering about Malraux and Veblen and Dube. Rodgers had emptied his wineglass twice. He said too much when he was drunk, or uneasy, and now he was both.

"You took the job?"

"Oh yes. Of course. I packed my books and papers and drove to Newton and taught two classes a week. A hundred and ninety-five dollars I was paid, plus faculty privileges."

"One ninety-five?"

"Plus faculty privileges. That was the royal business in those days. They had a faculty commissary and an indoor swimming pool. It was all very exciting. Someone had hired me on. That first job, you know. You're just happy to be there. You take nothing for granted. You haven't learned that yet." Rodgers reached for his wine.

He couldn't figure out whether the young man was compelled or merely indulging him. He had never been good on reactions. Those he had left to Connie.

"Newton was wild back then. Everything ran by consensus. The students were always protesting something, running around naked. Anyway, one night, about two months after I got there, the phone rang. It was late Saturday and I'd been to a party and, actually, I was stoned. Stoned out of my mind, actually." Rodgers lowered a make-believe sledgehammer onto his head. "That was another thing about Newton. There was some very good grass around. It just seemed to be around. I figured it was Connie calling. But the voice on the line was one I'd never heard before, this deep, official voice. 'Hello, Alex,' he said. 'This is Joseph Van Buskirk. I'm terribly sorry to be calling you so late.' I thought to myself: Who is Joseph Van Buskirk? The name sounded so familiar. 'As I say, Alex,' this Van Buskirk said to me, 'I hate to disturb you at home.' 'It's okay,' I told him. My mind was racing: *Van Buskirk, Van Buskirk.* Then it hit me: the president of the university! President Van Buskirk! This real Wall Street type. 'I'm afraid I'm going to need your help, Alex, in an extremely unpleasant task. One of your students, Mary Martin, has been in a car accident. There's really no choice in this.' 'No choice in what?' I said, and he said, 'We need you to identify the body.'

"My God. I mean, this was some strong grass I had smoked. Very strong. I could have handled a discussion with Connie. I maybe wanted to talk to her. But this was crazy. The president said, 'The problem is that we can't notify the next of kin, Alex, without someone to identify the body. We didn't want to ask one of her friends, you see. These situations can be very rough emotionally. There was no one else to call, really. She's just a first-year. You're her adviser. She's even in one of your classes.'

" 'The morning class,' I said.

"He jumped right on that. 'You know her, then? You'd be able to identify her?'

" 'I know what she looks like.'

" 'Good,' the president said. 'I'll be by in fifteen minutes.'

"Jesus. What does that mean? He'll be by? Does he have her in the trunk? No, that means he's going to have to drive me somewhere. I'm going to have to get into the car with him and we're going to have to drive somewhere. To a funeral parlor. I'm going to have to drive to a funeral parlor with him. To identify the body. I mean, this is how my mind is operating. All very scrambled. I'm trying to figure out whether I'm going to be able to keep it together, actually. Because if I can't, you know, if I somehow lose my cool in front of him or he picks up on my being stoned . . . I mean, that's it. No more job. My career ruined. You know how the mind can get under the influence of grass, that paranoia."

"Wait a second," Ken said. "Didn't she have any ID on her? Why did they need you?"

Rodgers shrugged. "I don't know, exactly. I never asked about that. It must have been a law, that someone who knew the victim had to inspect the body in person. All I knew was that the president wanted me there. It must have been some state law." Rodgers sipped his wine. "I lived in this little carriage house out in the country that I rented for sixty dollars a month, utilities included. If you can imagine. A quiet place. Peaceful. About five minutes later, I heard this car pull up on the gravel. It was much too soon. You know, when someone says fifteen minutes they usually mean half an hour. That's understood, isn't it? I felt ambushed, really. You don't tell someone fifteen minutes and then drive up five minutes later. I might not have been any more ready in fifteen minutes or half an hour, but at least

I would have had the chance to adjust to the idea. Wash my face, brush my teeth. Maybe it was fifteen minutes. But it didn't feel like it.

"Then I see these colored lights spinning outside my window. This car that's pulled up is a cop car. Now I know for sure that I'm fired. The president's going to pull up in his Rolls-Royce as I'm being led away by the cops, right? There's a knock on the door and I freeze. Just freeze. It's like one of those movies where you can hear the clock on the wall ticking. Tick tick tick. Except that I didn't have a clock. Maybe a minute goes by and there's another knock. This one louder. What choice do I have? I get up and open the door and there's President Van Buskirk, this big fat man in a black coat. He has this very concerned look on his face, very Walter Cronkite, and he's holding something in his hand. I swear to God for a second I thought it was a scythe. But it was just an umbrella. The cop car is behind him and it's raining and he looks at me and I look at him. I thought he might have smelled the grass. That was my concern. For a second neither one of us moves. He's sort of leaning in with his big Republican face, looking me over, and I'm figuring how I'm going to explain this to Connie, to my folks.

"'You'll need something more than that,' he says finally. 'It's a cold one.'

"So I get myself a coat and put that on and we walk out together and get into this car with three cops already in it. State troopers. With those shiny black knee boots. All three of them sitting there, not saying a word. I get in the backseat, between a trooper and the president, and there's two more in the front seat and I'm stoned out of my tree and we're going to identify Mary Martin's body. I mean, shit."

Ken said, "Why all the cops?"

"I don't know. I wondered about that later. Wouldn't one have been enough? Why all three? But there they were. Not one of them said hello. The driver started the car and we drove. I was still stoned. You couldn't have devised a worse place to put me. The troopers were looking at my clothes, jeans and some kind of leather fringe coat, and my hair. They knew what I'd been up to, I was sure of it. 'I hope I didn't wake you up,' the president said. 'Oh no,' I said. 'I was grading some papers.' 'On a Saturday night?' the president said. He whistled and the cop sitting next to me let out a chuckle. There was an awkward moment there, but the president smoothed right over it. 'I need to apologize again for this inconvenience, Alex. We're going to need to head to the morgue and get this over with. We should have you home in less than an hour.' I said, 'Sure.' 'I appreciate your being available.' 'Of course, I'm just sorry it's necessary,' I said.

"The driver, he must have been the commanding officer, he said, 'Goddamn shame is what it is. These kids. The risks they take.' He looked at me in the rearview mirror. 'They don't believe it can happen to them.'

"I said, 'What happened?'

"'Single-car accident. Out along 41. Driver drinking. Lost control of vehicle. Into a ravine. Passenger, this Martin girl, through the windshield. Into a tree. Broken neck. Dead on impact.'

"'What about the driver?' I said.

"'Oh, *him*,' the trooper said. 'He's fine.'

"'What a mess,' said the trooper next to me.

"'A real mess,' said the third trooper. 'A real mess job.'"

Rodgers paused and reached for his wine, then thought better of it. He could hear his son cooing at the baby from the other room: "What kind of girl does that? What kind of a silly girl?"

His son was obviously, stupidly smitten. He couldn't keep his hands off the baby. "Lambchop," he called her. "Love of my life." He carried her around in a ridiculous contraption, a sling that held the baby's back to his stomach, so that she hung there in front of him, her head bobbing absurdly. Rodgers could hear his son quack playfully as he changed her diaper in the next room.

His daughters, of course, had plopped the baby into his arms the moment they arrived and motioned with their hands, as if they were tossing salad. This meant he was to interact with her. There was about the act a kind of covert aggression; Rodgers felt as if he were being tested. *See here*, his daughters were saying. *Life goes on.*

But the infant felt inert in his arms, like a stony loaf of bread. He muttered one or two awkward words. As if sensing his discomfort, the baby squirmed with an alarming vitality. Rodgers feared he would drop her, briefly imagined the chaos that would ensue. The baby began to sputter, then to cry, its gums gleaming like tiny pink rinds. His daughter-in-law appeared immediately and swept the child away. "She's just hungry," his oldest daughter said, and they all agreed. Nonetheless, Rodgers felt humiliated by the entire episode. He wasn't Connie.

Ken said, "Cops never change."

Rodgers nodded. "Yeah. They just kept on like that. I was relieved, actually. I settled back and kept my mouth shut. The president was staring out the window, at the rain. He was a dapper fellow, but up close you could tell he'd had some acne as a kid. He had those scars. His hands were folded in his lap and his shoulders were tense. I guess he was scared, too."

"That must have sobered you up."

"Not really," Rodgers said. "My thoughts were coming too fast. What I was most worried about was that at some point I might start talking, you know? Really let loose and start blabbing. And then I might not be able to stop. You know how that can happen?"

"Sure," Ken said.

"I was already paranoid. I was sure the troopers, for instance, knew what I'd been up to. But we were trapped in this strange situation. What could they say? I started thinking about what was going to happen next, picturing things, planning it out, really. We were going to pull up to the funeral parlor—"

"Wasn't it a morgue?"

"Yes, that's right. It was. But somehow in imagining it, that's not what I saw." Rodgers smiled and the ball at the end of his nose flushed. "What I saw was this small-town funeral parlor, lit from within, sort of like one of those Hopper paintings. We'd walk in and there'd be this warm foyer with flowers and wreaths and things. Then we'd pass into another room, a kind of chapel, with pews for people to sit and a raised area for people to speak. And we might wait there for a few minutes. And they might bring us coffee. Then we'd move along into this back room and that's where they'd have the coffins. The bodies would all be neatly dressed and they would wheel Mary Martin over and I would look down at her, lying in this pink-padded coffin, and nod, and that would be it. I kept running this scenario through my head. The foyer, the chapel, the coffee."

"What's that theory of Malraux's? The assimilation of death?"

"Yes, the assimilation of death. The adjustments one makes, tries to make. That's what I must have been up to," Rodgers said. For a moment he saw Connie, saw her as she had appeared when he entered her study, lying under a blanket, her face set in the wax of motionless blood.

"How well did you know the student?" Ken said.

Rodgers shook his head and steadied his hands on the edge of the table. He wanted more wine but worried that he would spill. "Mary Martin? Oh, I barely knew her at all. She was a quiet girl. Quiet. She looked a bit like that actress, the one in *Love Story*. Pretty. Dark hair. But quiet."

The conversation in the other room hit a lull. There was just the occasional snap of the fire that his son had built earlier. Rodgers had forgotten how to open the flue, and suffered some gentle teasing over this. He listened, now, to the fire, and sat back and stared at the orange shadows cast along the doorway between the two rooms.

Mary Martin had spoken just once in his class. But he was alarmed to find the memory of this incident still very much alive. Rodgers had been lecturing on the Ik, an African tribe celebrated among cultural anthropologists for their meager standards of community. Mary Martin was in the back row, where she customarily sat. Gradually, as if with great effort, her pale face took on a disturbed animation.

"You mean they just leave one another to die?" she demanded.

"Oftentimes, yes."

"Even a relative, or a friend?"

"I'm afraid so."

Mary Martin shook her head and glared at him, as if he were somehow responsible for the Ik's behavior.

Rodgers tried to soften his approach: "It is true that the Ik represent an extreme, an affront to our conception of compassion. But every culture operates according to what Mead referred to as a concentricity of love. We all make decisions about whom we can afford to care for. In essence, we choose who to love. We do this every day, without even thinking about it. We might feel bad for a person, but that doesn't mean we choose to take care of him, to love him. We might pass by him every day without a thought. If any of you have been to Mexico, for instance, or India, you know it is impossible to move about without beggars asking for help, people who are in real need."

"But that's different," a second student said. "This tribe you're talking about—"

"The Ik."

"Yeah, the Ik. They leave their own relatives to die. Parents leave their *kids*."

"In some cases, yes. I know it's disturbing. But this is how they must lead their lives. They live in an extremely harsh environment and must make harsh decisions as to whom they can afford to love. Sometimes a father or mother decides there is only enough food for the two of them, and not for the children. Or they decide that a child is too sick to care for and, yes, they are left behind. But this is not cruelty. Weakness, perhaps. But not cruelty."

"You're saying it's not cruel to leave a kid like that?"

"No. What I'm saying is that the Ik, all of us, really, we possess only a finite amount of love, a finite amount of the internal resources by which we can enact demonstrations of our love. And in some cases, some people choose . . . they choose to love themselves, or to love each other, rather than their children."

Mary Martin sat at the back of the classroom, her jaw clamped. Rodgers fumbled on, but the rest of the lecture was a loss. He felt overruled, condemned by the dull contempt of her gaze.

Ken cleared his throat. He was staring steadily at Rodgers. "Are you okay?"

"Yes. Certainly."

"Did you want to finish your story?"

"My story?"

"Yeah. Did you ever ID the body?"

"Oh yes. Yes. Where was I? In the car? Okay. In the car with the president and the troopers, right?" Rodgers motioned toward the wine and tapped his brow. "We drove for a while, I know that. Then the car pulled up behind this building. It was low brick, with a concrete ramp and a doorway. I thought for a minute it must be some kind of errand one of the troopers had to run, because it was clearly the back entrance. The lot was unpaved. The president said, 'Let's get this over with,' and got out. The cops got out, too. I looked through the window and saw these bright circles of light pouring through the doorway, and at the center of these circles at the top of the ramp was a gurney and on top of that was the body, this white body lying there looking very small. The president crouched down and stuck his big face in the window and said, 'Are you ready, son?' and I got out. The troopers fell in around me, as if I were a suspect, or some personage worthy of protection, and they marched me up the ramp and to the doorway and I looked down."

"Jesus," Ken said.

"Jesus is right." It was infuriating, what he'd been asked to do. He could see that now. What right had anyone, even puffy old President Van Buskirk, to drag him into this? He was a young adjunct, with a pretty fiancée, not so many years older than his students. It was Saturday night, late. He had been sitting at home, innocently, waiting for her to call, to hear her voice. He had nothing to do with any of this. He remembered, particularly, how bright it all was, how he had been forced up the ramp, like a suspect.

"I looked down. She was in awful shape. A real mess job, as the trooper put it. They had her naked there and you could see one of her ribs, the end of it, poking through. Her eyes were closed and

I remember that one of the orderlies reached down and opened them and in the same motion he pulled her jaw up. Because, you see, her jaw was broken, hanging loose there; he did this so I'd be able to recognize her. The other orderly said: 'Is this the woman you know to be Mary Martin?' I couldn't speak. I nodded and turned away. But then this same orderly said, 'I'm sorry, sir, we need you to be quite certain. Could you please look again?' I started to feel sick. It wasn't the blood. They'd cleaned the blood off. But there were these places where you could see the fat, these yellowish gashes, and her face . . . I mean, it had to be held together. They hadn't given me any chance to adjust, was the thing. It was just: out of the car and up the ramp and yes or no."

"Jesus," Ken said again.

"I kept looking at her, this young girl, and thinking: That's her. She's dead. She isn't coming back. But I couldn't really believe it, not emotionally. It didn't register."

"You must have been protecting yourself."

"Right. Sure." Rodgers nodded. He was trying to remember why he had started this story. Perhaps he had meant to convey a mood of boyish exhilaration, that sense of possibility that belongs to the young. But this was not how he felt. Rather the opposite. He ran a finger under the collar of his new turtleneck, a gift from the girls. A drop of sweat traced his ribs. How had his home become so ungodly hot?

Ken said something more about the police and their ill habits. Rodgers listened to his children in front of the fire. They were worrying over the baby. His daughters were noting, for perhaps the hundredth time, how much she resembled Connie.

Just before dinner, in fact, they had converged outside his study and yammered on about the likeness. The same button chin and generous forehead. Wasn't it uncanny? Rodgers had stooped over his desk and felt a pulse of rage bang bloodily behind his eyes. He imagined storming into the hallway and telling them what he really thought: that the child, with its drooping cheeks and fat lips, looked like a little Jewish gangster. That he half expected a cigar to be poking from the corner of its mouth.

In moments such as these, he wanted nothing more than the peace of an empty house, an end to the polite dismay his children forced onto him.

It was expected he would join them soon, and find his place at the edge of them, his two daughters and his son with the new baby. But he knew, without a strong sense of wanting to know, that he would not be terribly missed if he stayed put.

It was not that he didn't love his children. He did. There were photos all around, photos with the right sorts of smiles, or nearly so. But he had always felt overmatched by the demands of their love, the red wailing and grubby hands and later the expectant gazes and sullen protests. It was Connie to whom he ceded a true concern. And she who had run interference between him and the world of his deficiencies.

He could hear her, the soft lilt of her voice, as she stood at the stove and hummed a Beatles song, that one about a silver hammer. If Connie had been there, with him in Newton, she would have known how to handle the situation with Mary Martin, how to undo his panic. He wouldn't have been stoned in the first place, if she had been there. Or he might never have answered the phone. And if she were here, tonight, he would be in the other room with her, with their children, together. She was the one who made that possible, coaxed from him feelings that brought him closer to the center of things.

Ken shook his head. "That's a crazy story," he said. "Crazy."

Rodgers said nothing. He had thought to answer, but found he could not. The feeling was not one of drowning, more that the breath had been sucked out of him. He was seized by the urge to tear his new turtleneck off, felt this might ease his breathing, cool his skin, though he merely looked to the table in hope of finding water there.

"We should probably join the others, huh?" Ken said.

"Yes, of course."

The young man got up and offered an awkward wave and left.

Rodgers listened absently to the discussion in the other room. "Where've you been?" his son asked Ken, and Ken murmured something and the group laughed. "Maybe we should make him drink wine more often," his son said. Then the group discussed plans for the next day. A late brunch, a trip to the nautical museum. The baby began to cry and was given over to her mother to be fed. There was a momentary humming. Rodgers knew that his absence was being charted.

Those last months had been so quiet. The children were gone, sunk into hectic lives and cowed, truthfully, by their mother's illness, or perhaps afraid to interfere with his grief. They had proved adept, this last year, at matching him silence for silence. Their conversations remained stiff, and a little hollow. They made him wonder: Is this all there is to fatherhood, or have I missed something?

Connie had been dreadfully quiet. She spent mornings by the sun window, perched in her favorite rocking chair, and afternoons sleeping in the den. She moved with the deliberation of one who hopes to obscure suffering. Rodgers watched her grow gaunt. He felt, in her presence, small and boneless.

In moments of duress, such as after treatments, he adjusted pillows and said the right words, but these somehow had the effect

of underscoring the unnaturalness of his attempts. Knowing her
affinity for sun, he cursed the gray days of autumn until he felt his
throat rip.

And then the study; that afternoon in the study. She had done
well the previous day, eaten all her potatoes and even a bite or two
of chicken. In the morning he had seen a trace of color in her face.
To find her like that, still and unbreathing, her hand clenched against
her white cheek—he simply shut down. It was only the phone calls
and later a visit from his neighbor that allowed things to move
forward.

One by one his children came into the kitchen until he was
surrounded. They were here now, his sweet son and daughters, asking what was wrong and their voices, all going at once, composed a
child's chant. "Are-you-okay-are-you-okay-Dad-what-is-it-Dad-
what-is-it?" He tried to tell them, "Don't be scared," but could not.
He understood that it was his role, as father, to provide some reas-
surance, to subdue the tide of sorrow that now threatened them all.
It was only this business of breath that held him back, the loss of
breath.

To calm himself, Rodgers closed his eyes. The baby was whim-
pering and Ken was apologizing and someone was stroking his poor
old bald head and the youngest, Amy, she was even weeping. He
felt hands being laid upon him, one pair then another, the hot cling
of his children's fingers. They were good children, more than he
deserved, because within them lived some link to her; it was this link
to which he attached his hopes.

There was quite a lot of commotion, you would have to say
that, a lot of crying, a lot of noise, and he could feel his children
crowding in on him and he heard the baby nearby, crying now, and
he must have reached out for her or made some indication of his

need, because someone placed her in his lap. Rodgers opened his eyes. She stared up at him with sleepy eyes, a tiny fist worked loose from her swaddling and pressed against her cheek. Rodgers examined the intricacy of her face and hands and straightened up a bit and then quietly said, "Why do these crazy people cry so much? Can you tell me that? Why is everybody crying so much, baby girl?"

Geek Player, Love Slayer

Computer Boy swaggers over to my cube to help me open this one knucklehead email Phoenix sent me and within about, oh, two seconds, I'm ready to whip off his khakis and blow him right there. He's leaning over my keyboard, tappy-tap-tap, with his lousy beautiful sideburns and his Right Guard wafting all over the place, and underneath that this kind of wounded musk that tends to make my nipples go *boing*, and his teeth which I could fucking eat they look so healthy. I have, mind you, already offered him my seat. But he can't allow that. No-no-no. Don't you move your pretty little self, he tells me, which is when neighbor Brisby starts snarking away and I'm like, Oh for Chrissakes, why does this obnoxious creature, this dopey slab of masculine grace, whose name is (try not to laugh) Lance, and whom I have taken to calling Lancelot, Sir Lance-me-a-lot, why does this totally throat-lickable hottie have to be such a shitbrain?

So I just sit there smelling him and watching his unreasonably defined triceps pulse and unpulse and noticing the blond hairs on his earlobe, like tiny spears of wheat, and the way his firm little rump tenses up when he gets a systems error. And the worst part of it is that he keeps running these lines about how I must be doing something to my machine, my keystrokes must be pretty vigorous—key-

strokes, get it?—and even though I'm actually kind of impressed by his use of the word *vigorous,* there's no way I can flirt back without losing total office cred with Brisby, who's outright laughing at this point. It's not like I have time for this crap anyway; I'm on deadline. Though actually, the worst part is my leched-out imagination, wherein Lancelot is bending me like a band saw and this can't be happening, *this cannot be happening.* I cannot be lusting after the Computer Boy on deadline, that is too lame for even me.

Only now Brisby's on the phone with his fiancée, for the twelfth fucking time this hour, and Lancey tells me he's going to have to reboot and suddenly *down he goes,* under my desk, and I forget to skootch my chair back because I'm too busy staring at his back and counting up the individual muscle groups, sort of flowcharting them, and then something rubs against my knee, his wrist I guess, but of course I've got these jeans on, because it's forty fucking degrees in the office; the hotter it gets outside, the colder they keep the office. Then, just to balance himself I suppose, Lancey sets his hand on the bridge of my foot and starts in with these little appraising squeezes, like he's fitting me for a pair of pumps, and I want to tell him, Hey, bright boy: there's a whole calf and thigh where that came from! But before I can say anything, he turns and informs me *I've got real soul* and I want to barf and run my tongue along the pink canals behind his ears all at once and I can hear Brisby mumbling his I-love-yous and hanging up and my screen goes blank. Lancey rolls back on his haunches just enough to send a ripple under his shirt and I imagine looping my arms around him, taking the meat of his shoulders in my palms, and his front teeth, his, let me emphasize, *goddamn perfect front teeth,* biting my clavicle, and I know Brisby's going to slag me for the rest of eternity, until death do us part, but it's too late, I'm halfway off my chair in a canine posture and my knees are trembling.

Ahem.

You're all set, Lance tells me. Just turn it on. He's back to hovering over me. You know how to turn it on, don't you, he says. I'm like, Yeah, it's not the turning on I'm worried about. It's keeping the hard drive going. And immediately, even before Brisby snarks, I regret having reduced myself to lurid banter with Computer Boy, who gives me his cheap and evil grin, causing this adorable declivity in his left cheek, not exactly a dimple, a crimp, a *crimple*, which he then has to ruin by saying: Maybe you could come back to my office sometime and we could *work on that.* And now, paddling to regain my footing and really hoping he'll just leave me be, I mutter: Yeah, maybe when the new laptops come in, Lance, I could come back there and give you my special laptop dance.

I'd like that, he says, I'd like that *very much,* then—get this—*winks,* so that finally I can muster a decently derisive laugh, a true ho-ho-ho-you-bonehead-why-don't-you-crawl-back-to-whatever-mousepad-you-came-from kind of laugh, which still isn't enough to get Brisby off my back, because the instant Computer Boy and his filet mignon of an ass have bounced off he messages me: *When do I get mine?* Meaning, laptop dance, the prick.

What I really want to know is when this sad new genre of human being, the Geek Player, came into existence. Because even two years ago the Systems Manager was this little smudge of a person who frittered on about mainframe systems and was perfectly content to hang with his tech buddies and flirt with the forty-something divorcées at Mac Warehouse. Those guys had a certain pathetic, introverted arrogance, because they knew they had the rest of the office by the stones. But they were basically *frightened of people.* Then this new breed started up, guys like Lance, who are no longer Systems Managers. Now they're Computer Guys, which means they can be cute and outgoing and some of them, such as Lance, even ripped. And they strut around the office, coming to the rescue of all us computer fuckups, including the publisher, whose dome turns the color of salsa whenever his Mac crashes and who worships the very ground Lance walks on, because without Lance his *cursor won't move.* When he isn't hustling the chicks in production and advertising and even that one chick in editorial (me), when he isn't out amongst his subjects, in other words, Lance sits in his office talking to the other Geek Players in the other offices, on speaker phone, all of them hollering, and playing Nerf basketball via remote, and cheating.

How did Computer Guy become the Lifeguard of the decade? How did the mild-mannered Systems Manager morph into an omnipotent Geek Player, Love Slayer? Brisby and I have developed the following theories:

Geekerella: The existing SM population, recognizing player potential, has undergone an eerie Men's Magazine transformation involving facial scrapes, free weights, some kind of Toastmasters public-speech seminar, and clothing from Structure.

Trickle-down chic: Noting the wealth and power afforded anyone with a whiff of tech know-how, an entirely new population of vaguely cool and mendacious men (previously drawn toward, say, condo sales) has chosen a career in the computer sciences.

Not-so-great expectations: The general population, steeped in the greasy autism of the Systems Manager, has a tendency to inflate the coolness of the Computer Guy. As Brisby puts it: When you're expecting Bill Gates, Steve Jobs starts looking like Brad Pitt. A related phenomenon (*The Naughty Wonk Effect*) holds that a geek overlay accentuates sexiness through irony, the same principle that leads pornographers to script so many gang-bang scenes featuring librarians.

But how far will this paradigm shift go? Geek mafioso? Geek supermodels? Geek gangsta rap? How much cultural power will the Geek Player amass before people realize he's just a guy who can *talk to machines*? And, perhaps more to the point, why do Computer Boy and his crimple have to haunt my every waking moment?

So we're at one of these office-wide happy-hour deals, which are supposed to build company morale, though what they tend to do is reinforce the sense, at least between Brisby and myself, that we are being *bribed into silence*. Of course Brisby ducks off to some fiancée-engineered function, like the good little monogamous soldier he is, leaving me fully vulnerable to the forces of office tooldom, against which I have only drunkenness as a defense, so that when something lands on my hair I flail around in this slightly trashed girlie spasm and smack into what feels like a tree limb with skin. There's Computer Boy and his cinematic teeth and he does this drowsy thing with his eyelids, some kind of demiwink, which makes him look like a cat in the sun.

Ciao bella, he says. Did I scare you?

I thought you were a fly, I say.

Maybe I am. Maybe I'm a Spanish fly.

Oh please, I say. Go ask the wizard for a brain.

Which you might figure would shut his piehole. But no, he has to speak, some ridiculous I-don't-even-know-what rap about, oh Christ, *something.*

What happened to your fan club? I say. For the last hour Marcie the Production Ho has been shoving her C-cups in his face and even as we speak she's across the room sending me the official that-my-man death rays, which only makes the whole thing more pathetic, because there's no angle in competing with a chick who lists nipple piercing on her résumé under *Other Skills.*

What are you drinking, he says.

G&T.

He shakes his sweet, vacant head.

Gin, I say slowly, and tonic.

Gin, he says. Does that make you want to sin?

Actually, it makes me want to chop your head off. Does that qualify as a sin? Or is that more like a public service?

But good old Lancey, he's not one to give up too easy. He keeps asking questions. Like he read a book once that said: Ask lots of questions. Chicks dig it when you take an interest in their lives. When did I start at the paper? How did I get into reporting? Where do I live? You can tell he's not really listening, which neither am I, thanks to the drinks.

Then he starts this whole touching my hair thing, playing with my hair, and I tell him to knock it off, not very convincingly. His eyes droop a little and he shoots me his *look of false contrition,* but in such a way that rather than noticing how supposedly sorry he feels, what I notice is the muscles flaring out from his neck, these twin blades of muscle, almost like gills. Jesus, does Lancey work out his neck? Does he go to the gym with a specific neck regimen? It occurs to me in this horrible flash I'd prefer not to classify as an epiphany that he's probably strong enough to bench press my entire (naked) body with his neck. I could plop myself down on his upturned face, his wet, white teeth, and he could neck-press me.

I look around helplessly for Brisby or someone else from editorial, who'll snicker the whole thing away. But there's no one left except the horny ad rats in their commission grins and the sulky face-mangled production scum. Marcie? Where the hell is *Marcie*?

Computer Boy moves in for the kill and I can smell the white Russians on his breath, sweet and milky and boozy and his rotten cologne/deodorant and his gorgeous throat pullying away as he swallows. But just as I'm about to be carried off onto the sea of stupid love, this little yeoman of respectability tosses me a line and I say: How old are you? Tell me how old you are.

How old do you *think* I am?

I don't know, Lance. Seven?

Twenty-seven, he says. In December. Why, how old are you?

Which, I mean, how can you reach twenty-seven in this culture without figuring out that this is a *bad* question? How does that happen?

Where do you live? I say.

This question seems to spook him. He runs a hand through his hair, which crackles, and shows me his biceps with the two veins that intersect like rural routes on a map, hoping I'll be so mesmerized as to forget my question.

Around here, he says, gesturing vaguely.

Really? I bite into my lime. Where?

Now he leans back, looking much less sure of himself, running my hair through his thumb and forefinger, like a suit he's considering. Yeah, he says, I got this box right behind the bar. It's pretty cool. I never have to worry about DUIs.

A response so lame that I'm sort of rooting for him to not be speaking English anymore. And it dawns on me, falls on me actually, as bricks fall upon the naive from a great height: Lancey lives with his parents. A twenty-seven–year-old dependent. His hulking Computer Boy bod cramped onto a single bed, Cheryl Tiegs tacked to the wall, Rubik's cube on the dresser, mom bustling into his room with his underwear washed and folded into little squares, making him macaroni and cheese, dad yelling at him to take out the garbage. Only the great sadness of this realization rescues me from the competing desire to start chewing his lips, which, thank god, before I can do this Marcie knifes her way over, all miffed and studded, and I peel off to the bathroom before anything catty can happen and sit and listen to my bladder empty of tonic and wonder why Brisby couldn't have stuck around long enough to save me from myself.

I'm talking to Gala about this shit, because she knows my whole deal, every hopeful seems-like-a-nice-guy-really-smart-kissed-me-goodnight flameout, and I tell her, There's no way I can give him the goods now, right? Right, Gala? If he's living at home?

Why not? she says.

It's, just, like a rule, right? Didn't we have that rule?

But Gala, though my best friend in the world, is maybe not the best person to consult, because five months ago she caught her husband cheating and gave him the boot, and the whole thing's made her less sure of everything. She used to give me these stern speeches about not treating my body like a disposable washcloth; pride in ownership and so forth. Now, she just asks: Well, what do you *want* to do?

I want to fuck him silly, I say. Oh my god, Gala, you have no idea. I was on my way to lunch today and he was sitting there on the floor of his office with these parts all around him and this big screwdriver and these forearms.

A handyman, Gala says.

A handyman who lives with this parents.

You don't know that.

That's what all the strutting is about, I say. *Overcompensation.*

Maybe the strutting is just strutting. Maybe he's hung, Gala says.

Which, I mean: How did we get from *disposable washcloth* to *hung?*

Call him, Gala says. You've got a phone list, right? Just call him.

What if his mom answers? What am I supposed say: Hello ma'am. You don't know me, but I want to lick your son's balls. Is he expected home later?

A door slams over at her place and my godson, Justin (who is so cute I would actually eat him if not monitored), comes howling in. Gala tells me to hang on a sec and yells at Justin to please go into the other room, mommy's talking to someone on the phone right now, which makes me feel very much like a depraved auntie.

He does know this computer stuff, I say, so he's got to have some kind of an intellect, right? Besides, I've always been kind of a geek, haven't I Gal? In school. Wasn't I always kind of a geek?

But Justin's going crazy now, hollering something about pizza, daddy gives him pizza, he wants pizza. He's such a little *man* I want to laugh, though actually what happens is I start crying a little bit, thinking about Gala and how she looked in her bridal gown, how she gazed at John during their first dance, with such dreamy trust that me and the other bridesmaids could feel the hammering of our hearts. Not that marriage is any bowl of mousse, but at a certain point you realize it's better than tearing around town with the big scarlet *Un* on your chest. Getting involved with guys who are either dogs outright or else sensitive guys, which just means their molten core of misogyny is buried a little deeper, takes a little longer to get to, that place where you're eating breakfast at some lousy diner after a night of wild angry sex, at-least-we-still-have-this sex, or no sex at all, and you want to ask him: *What happened to that other thing we had?* But he's looking down at his plate, hacking up a waffle, and his face is like a cursor, a dead blink, so you just ask him to pass the syrup.

Only it's worse than that, because maybe it's not them at all. Maybe it's me. Maybe I'm the one who somehow fucks it up, demands too much, needs too much, gets too angry, weepy, moody. Maybe I'm unlovable is the truth, and I plunge into one of those moments where I can see everything I'm never going to get—the guy, the dress, the one dance—and Justin's wailing away and Gala says she has to go, so I hang up.

Brisby and me are heading out for some tacos, but the elevator's taking forever and the whole office seems trapped under a glaze of late-afternoon discontent, except for Computer Boy, who we can hear laughing, one of those insincere machine-gun laughs—*chut-chut-chut*—like the modern-rock jocks do all the time. Brisby looks at me and we drift toward his little tittie-poster-festooned office. It's not like we're eavesdropping either, because he's practically shouting: *No way, dude! She looked like ass. What were her stats, dude? You fucking liar! She was fucking bacterial! Chut-chut-chut. Yeah, if it was me, I'd send that shit out for dry-cleaning! Wait, where'd you find that? In the crack? Bleach, dude! Clorox! Chut-chut-chut. I'm fuckin' serious, dude. That shit will make you go blind. Penicillin, dude. Penis chillin. Chut-chut-chut.*

And what's remarkable is not that someone who has been alive for nearly three decades would speak like this (though that is kind of remarkable) but that it goes on and on and on, this proto-fratboy-speak that's not so much offensive after a while as sad, imbued with the deep lonely rage of the Geek Player.

All Brisby and I can say in the elevator is: Wow.

I work up a few *chut-chut*s over lunch, but Brisby wants to talk about his fiancée, whom I've met twice and who seems cool, kind of pretty in a J. Crew way, maybe a little on the uptight side. She wants Brisby to take these classes before they get married, is the latest issue, with her priest. (She has a *priest!*) This will bring them closer together, she figures, which I'm not so sure about, because Brisby's not a churchy kind of guy. Even after his mom had a stroke and he had to move back from Dallas, you didn't hear him talking about God's Great Plan or any of that crapola. He just said: What am I supposed to do, let her drown in drool?

But now he's looking at me, the poor guy, like what do I think he should do. Suddenly I feel flustered. What are the priest's stats? I say.

Brisby goes into his Morley Safer face, the one he uses when he's got some bigwig on the phone, and for a sec I'm afraid I've pissed him off.

He's not currently bacterial, Brisby says. I know that.

Is his penis chillin? Do you know if his penis is chillin?

Shit. Brisby smacks his forehead. I forgot to ask.

And just sitting there, munching on our tacos, with sour cream painting our lips and hot sauce burning our throats, I'm so relieved Brisby is around, that he's a friend of mine. That we heard Computer Boy together so that he can provide, if not moral guidance, at least a foretaste of the devout shame I would experience post-bop.

*   *   *

Then it's Halloween, which means the paper throws one of these mandatory costume parties intended to lube up the advertisers. I figure, what the hell, it's a Saturday night, I'm not getting any younger, so I go as Lolita: kneesocks, pleated skirt, twin braids, and the dogs of this world howl and howl; there's something about the prospect of boffing a twelve-year-old that sends the sperm count into orbit.

Plenty of booze and some decent grilled shrimp appetizers and a DJ who somehow manages to not suck. The little club they've rented out, Sub Rosa, has this tiny sunken dance floor, and all the chicks, me included, do their thing once management clears out, screaming along to "Got to Be Real" and "I Will Survive," shaking gynapalooza style, while the dweebs from business circle around fanning the flames, and the place actually starts to get a little sexy, a little sweaty, which is when Computer Boy makes his entrance. He's wearing this Zorro-meets-Liberace getup, raccoon mask, pinkie rings, a spangled cape that whips around as he vogues, and this big whoop goes up and us chickees tear off the cape and all he's wearing is a white leather vest and a matching *codpiece* and there it is, Der Weinerschnitzel, sitting up like a pleased little puppy. It all comes together now: he's a queen. A big flaming murder-'em-with-my-abs queen. Perfect.

Then his date appears, Marcie the Production Ho, trussed up in a tit-spiller, buried under blue eye shadow, and throwing sass. The pair of them, what a freak show, like Rocky Horror without the singalong.

But what the hell! The music's good and the gin's cast a certain forgiving silliness onto everything and I'm enjoying flailing around in the belief of my sexiness, which is being reinforced by the menfolk, who ask me if I'm a naughty girl and do I want detention and paw my skirt and gaze upon my hair like it's a divine accomplishment. I mean, how many of these nights does one get, anyway?

I can feel Brisby checking me out from the edge of the room, where he and fiancée are poking at the remains of the appetizers. They're both dressed in prison stripes and dopey little hats, with a little plastic ball and chain between them (get it?) and it's obvious Elle Elle Bean is in one of her snits, wants out of here, away from the depravity, and even though Brisby is probably my last link to common sense, to my not doing something marvelous and stupid, I'm ready for them to ship off into their goddamn bloodless duet of a life and leave the rest of us to gobble each other up. What it is: I don't like the look on Brisby's face, so glum and smug that I want to walk over there and slap him, though before I can even take a step in that direction, he's gone. Of course.

I turn back to the party and there's Lancelot, launching into this exuberant B-boy Pentium Chip dance routine, which is sexy in a Tourettesy sort of way, and highly effective as a herding strategy. He backs me into this dark, quiet corner with his goddamn sensational cock of a cock, away from the music but still in plain view, and I can feel the booze thickening my tongue, my resistance going to pudding.

Where's your date? I say weakly.

He looks around. Who? Marcie? Yeah, she looks cool, huh?

Very escort service, I say. Very STD.

I don't see your partner in crime, he says. What's his name? Bixby?

Which almost makes me laugh, because Lancey obviously thinks we're a thing, he's that out to lunch. But before I can make the next crack, he takes a step forward so that he's actually, um, against me.

You're cool, he says. You know that? I like you.

For just a second I step back from the situation and look at this dumb brute in what amounts to cut-rate lederhosen and try to figure out whatever happened to subtlety, restraint, courtship, the wise gentle dance of desire against its tether. Then Lancelot leans down and presses his mouth against mine, and his lips are soft and wet on the inside and I can taste the Geek Player Binaca on his breath as he nibbles his way into my mouth, and his body grinds against mine, warm and hard. We start macking right there, in front of more or less everyone, so that I am magically reduced from Prepubescent Catholic School Girl to Office Slut and what's more, I'm *happy* about this, because I can feel his complicated grid of back muscles, his thighs, the silk of his armpit hair and I realize that even though this experience is total bullshit, it's also absolutely perfect, like in the movies, one of those deals where our differences are actually complementary and everyone goes: Oh, of course, why didn't we see it all along? They're *soul mates.* As opposed to real life where they say: You let him put his tongue *where?*

Here in the veiny arms of Lance the Computer Boy, I'm ready to surrender the idea of the perfect guy, someone I can talk to about anything on earth, because, really, in the end, isn't talk sort of overrated? Isn't talk just a way of pushing some romantic agenda that never works anyway? And besides, I could learn to speak computer, all those ones and zeroes, and I might even be able to train Lancey to burp with his mouth shut and not say *skank* so much, and having kids will settle him down; I sense he'll be a good father, because I can feel already how much he appreciates the maternal role, just by the way he keeps kneading my hips, like a Lamaze coach.

Then there's this loud *pop* and a fuzzy static sound and the music goes dead and the entire room turns on us, like we somehow dry-humped the music into silence, which, as it turns out . . . that little ledge against which I was seeking added pestle leverage seems to have been, in fact, an outlet. Nay, the very outlet into which DJ Dennis (DJ Dennis?) plugged his suspiciously karaoke-compatible DK2 Partymaster system.

Reentry into the world of the dwindling party would be shitty enough, but old Lancelot just has to complete the show by calling out, Thanks for the dance, babe! before ducking behind the appetizer table in an effort to conceal his *raging shaft of manhood.*

On the plus side is the fact that Marcie the Production Ho has taken X, rendering her unable to do anything worse than hug me fiercely and offer to pierce my septum.

I slip outside, into the lousy mucky air. Everyone watches me leave, the slutty aging reporter chick, which, if I were still drunk, might actually be a step up from aging reporter chick. But the booze is all through with my blood; it's coming off in acetone fumes, and the parking lot is empty and I'm leaving alone.

I don't want to worry about what anyone else thinks of me, because that's not the point. It's that I'm worried about what *I* think of me, what's become of me, why am I spending these precious years I'd always dreamed would involve a good man and a marriage and a little kid or two, why am I spending these years mooning over some smoothie from the Kingdom of Cheese?

This red Tercel tears into the lot, which is weird, because Brisby drives a red Tercel, and then Brisby himself lunges out of the car, still in his prisoner's outfit, and heads for the club, looking strangely pissed off, his little plastic chain dragging on the ground behind him. He must have forgotten something, keys or wallet. He's always forgetting something. A minute later he comes out again and I duck behind this pillar thing, but I can hear him crossing the lot and just the imagined sight of him, his goofy walk, his mouth pinched at the corners, the disappointment in his eyes, that alone is enough to start me blubbering. By the time he reaches me, I've collapsed into his arms and I'm sobbing, Sorry. I'm sorry. It's not my fault I fell for Computer Boy. I didn't mean to. But he's cute and he likes me and I'm not getting any younger, Bris. I'm thirty-fucking-three years old, you know? And besides, besides, you weren't there. You were supposed to save me. You were supposed to keep me from doing something stupid. What was I supposed to do without you there?

I'm not sure how much of this is intelligible, though, because my head is buried in his chest and the words are coming out all snotty. Brisby puts his arms around me and tells me it's okay, *shhh*, it's okay, and strokes my hair. I was just worried about you, he says. That's all. You had a lot to drink.

Then he lets me cry until I'm all done crying.

Maybe we could get some coffee, he says finally. Okay?

And it's such a sweet gesture, so much what I want. Just to sit there and sober up and shoot the shit with Brisby. What about Christine? I say. Won't she be waiting up?

Brisby looks down for a sec, shakes his head. Don't worry about it.

Is everything cool? I say.

And now I can see him struggling to keep *his* game face on. He reaches down and jerks at the plastic chain around his ankle. What a stupid costume, he says. I should have come as Unsightly Grout Fungus, like I originally planned.

The stripes make you look taller, I say.

I guess. It wasn't my idea.

He's still got his arms around me, loose, but not too loose, and I keep thinking how this should be awkward, the way our bodies are touching, because we're such pals. Then Brisby does this wonderful thing. He takes his thumb and forefinger and gently lifts my chin and presses his lips to my forehead and keeps them there for a minute, breathing through his nose. And I don't know what this means exactly; Brisby's holding me and there being nothing awkward about it, him holding me and saying *shhhh*, his breath flowing into my hair, the two of us on our way to get coffee, to talk, but not talking yet, just standing there in this empty parking lot, swaying, and that's all.

The Last Single Days of Don Viktor Potapenko

The Don had hit a slump. You could see it in his step. "Like a hurdy-gurdy man," said Peck, the Bitter Bartender. "Like a guy who works as a fucking monkey keeper." Peck did a little jig behind the counter. No one paid attention. "What'd he ever do?" Peck said. "You tell me."

It wasn't that bad, though really, it was.

The Don's whole thing was fluidity. He'd glide into the bar at ten on the nose, flip a cig from his palm onto his bottom lip and let it rest there a moment while, with his other hand, he drew a pewter lighter from his cape, snicked the flame to the business end and breathed in, nice and slow. Then he'd exhale and scratch the whiskers that ran along his jaw. He looked slightly blue and debonair, like a man on top of things, with a line of people waiting for answers only he could supply.

I loved The Don, loved his sophistication, his belief in sophistication, the part of him that seemed unflappable. He ordered Cuba Libres as a rule, whiskey sours if he'd had a bum day on the boardwalk. He knew how to dance, every step you could think of, and he knew how to behave around women. Or acted as if he did, which seemed to me the same thing in those days.

"Who's the action?" he'd say.

And I'd tell him: the sullen blond screwed to her stool after a tangle with her boyfriend, the pair of nurses drinking off their shift, a sandaled tourist gazing wistfully into her Manhattan.

"Who wants to be in my mouth?" The Don would say. "Who wants to be in The Don's mouth?"

"The blond?"

"Nurse with the big ass. Nurse with the big ass. Remember, Pancho: Not the prettiest. The sexiest. It's a mystery," he'd tell me. "But she's the one wants in. Look at how she holds the bottle, okay? That bottle's like my cock, okay? Not as thick as my cock, okay? But same idea."

I'd gaze at the plump nurse, marooned over her Heineken, and try to envision her in some ridiculous posture of abandon.

"Come on," he'd say. "It's obvious."

But now the problem was the Romanians. They wanted The Don to marry some cousin of theirs, for immigration purposes, he said. She was a quivery thing, no bigger than a matchstick, with a hat that looked like a tasseled lamp shade. They hustled her into the bar one time, handling her like a package they very much wanted to be rid of. The Don ducked out the back.

These men had returned a few times, bladelike in leather blazers. They ordered drinks and tried to look composed, pressing the heels of their hands against the bar, checking the clock, joking back and forth. Then they smashed their glasses on the ground and threw money at Peck.

"Fucking Romas," Peck said. "Fucking Roma tomatoes." Though not too loud. The owner was Romanian too.

"Busboy," Peck said. "Get your lazy ass over here. Bring your girlfriend, broom."

That was me. I was the busboy.

Obviously, this arrangement was cramping The Don's style, cutting his action, knocking his buzz. "What kind of plan is that?" he said. "Tracking me as if I were a common criminal."

"You are," Peck said.

"They really smashed their glasses?"

"Smasharoo," Peck said. "Smasharino."

The Don took a pull on his Cuba Libre. Brown dripped from his mustache. "You think this is going to rattle me? You think that?"

Peck finished watering the vodka, and fingered the nipple. Sometimes, after hours, I'd catch him absently sucking on one; not for the booze, just for the sensation. He had sores like cherry gumdrops around his mouth. His listening skills were zilch. He'd become bartender because his predecessor had stabbed Scoonie, one of the regulars. Before that, Peck had been the busboy.

"You think I'm rattled?" The Don said again.

"Like a jig's dice," Peck said. "Yeah."

"Put a fin on that?"

"Make it a deuce."

The Don winced quickly and scissored an oniony twenty onto the bar. He produced an eel-skin pouch embossed with the letters DVP—Peck claimed The Don had lifted this from a Vermont state senator on a gimlet tour of the area. He placed a shaving mirror on the bar and whisked his mustache with a dainty comb, like he was flicking off crumbs. He dipped his pinkie in a tin of beeswax and smoothed down each felty eyebrow, his movements crisp, somehow superstitious.

"It's how you look in profile," he told his reflection. "Just who you are, that thing you have; sex all over you. What can she do? What choice does she have, Don? She wants in the mouth. Let her in, Don. Let her in."

So sailed The Don, under his own wind, away from Peck and toward his intended, a sunstruck midwesterner with a froth of ginger hair. She wore a sundress and a lavender bra whose straps hugged the balls of her shoulders like a holster. What The Don called a real *Minerva*. He bowed before taking a seat, and smiled. (Peck especially hated The Don's teeth; Peck whose teeth looked like dried lemon seeds.)

They talked for a while, The Don mostly, asking questions in that way he had, his eyelids droopy with some shared sorrow, his mouth producing soft puffs of empathy. He lit her menthol 100s and told her about how this joint used to be owned by Meyer Lansky, how there's a dent in the backroom where the great man himself kicked in the plaster after a visit from the IRS.

Except that the Romanians had him spooked. Every time the door swung open he lost his place, the spell of seduction drifting up and leaving his hands behind, jittery as rabbits. He came to the bar for a third drink. Behind him, we could see Minerva stand abruptly and zip her purse.

Peck grinned his ghastly grin. "Here's a hint," he said. "You lose."

The Don assumed a look of monumental boredom. "Sappho's delight," he said, watching her lovely can swish away. "Isle of Lesbos."

"What're you saying? She's a dyke?" Peck laughed, a sound like tin being scraped. He sniffed The Don's twenty. "Plus ten and a half for the drinks, Casanova."

The door swung open and The Don, busy resculpting his hair, froze in the pose of a man with shampoo in his eyes. In walked Balanchine, one of the part-time drunks.

Peck laughed again. "Would you look at the guy? Like a ghost that just saw another ghost. Like, a bigger ghost."

It was hard for me to watch this: The Don's poise undone by fear. I felt he should be above fear.

"What happened?" Scoonie said. "You had her going."

"I told her she smelled smoky and sweet. Like cured bacon."

"Hint," Peck said. "Don't compare women to pork."

"Everybody loves bacon," The Don said quietly. "Show me who doesn't love bacon."

"Dumb," Peck said. "Dumb Don. Ask your boy."

I was counting lemons, one of many mindless duties Peck delighted in assigning me.

The Don said, "What do you know, Pancho?"

What *did* I know? I was nineteen years old, on the lam from college, a half step from ditching my old life for good. I was sure of very little; only that my parents had failed me somehow. It was a matter of getting far enough away to see things clearly. "Maybe she's kosher or something," I said. "I myself love bacon."

The Romanians were scary. They moved like men with concealed weapons, stiff in the wrong places, darker and thinner and somehow meaner than the Russian mobsters up the walk. They spoke a language that sounded argumentative and drunken, portending crude brands of violence.

Each week a bit more of The Don's sparkle faded. His nose began to twitch; his baritone faltered. Even the tourists who'd arrived in town hoping for foolish entanglement—the moussed, gum-murdering upstaters and shy Canadian divorcées, the slightly grubby au pair girls—began regarding him doubtfully.

The Don knew the only way out of his slump was to keep swinging, to swing until self-belief reattached itself and bore him up. On July Fourth, he hurried in, cape pressed, jawline gleaming. The Chamber of Commerce's dinky fireworks popped and cracked, streaking the front window.

"Tonight," The Don said. "Tell me about tonight."

But I didn't have to tell him anything. He spotted her immediately, and his beak dipped hungrily. A cancan girl from the Shuck 'n Jive called Aura. She had these wonderful Chinese eyes and a scalloped mouth. Her nose was no more than an elegant dollop. I liked to linger around her table, breathing the sweet bouquet of her body, flowery lotions and smoke.

"You know her?" I said. This seemed an amazing thing.

The Don settled across from her in profile. "I know," he said. "I know. I know. Don't mind me, okay? Don't listen. I'm just another soggy love letter from the isle of man. A woman of your beauty. Sure. I've seen you dance. Beautiful. Your hips have real carriage, real slide. But there's something missing. I'm wondering about that."

Aura looked at The Don like he was up past his bedtime.

"You've heard it all already, okay? So what's the harm? We're just a couple of pretty strangers passing time. Why the smirk? You don't think you're pretty? Okay. I know better than to make a fool of myself. Here's what I'm going to do: order a couple of drinks, put one in front of you. You do what you want. Dump it on my lap for all I care. You're enough of a knockout to pull it off. But there's still that thing, that missing thing."

I knew exactly what The Don meant. The same feeling kicked up inside me whenever my folks spoke about my future. It wasn't that they meant any harm, exactly, only that they had in mind a set of professions—estate planning was most often mentioned—whose blankness was the blankness of a prairie. But you see, I was drawn to the beach, the ocean's foamy brink, which smelled of salt and sex and reckless chances.

The Don gathered the drinks in his fingers, moving like in the old days, like corn stalks in a breeze, and slid her across the table. Ice clinked at the lip of the glass then fell back. To witness his execution, the way he carried himself, made me believe a glorious fate awaited me. I had only to watch carefully, to memorize certain moves, to absorb the attitude behind those moves.

He drew a finger down his nose. "Like I said, up to you. We're just talking. Talk talk. Call and response. Just keeping the ecosystem honest. It's all a negotiation anyway, okay? Someone like you can't be forced. All I'm saying is that you might be holding yourself back somehow. I'm enough of a goddamn failure to understand these things."

Aura looked up, amused now. "That sounds fair."

"Kapow. Right in the kisser." The Don tapped his chin in tribute. "What it is, I'm talking about dreams, Aura. Those ideas you have when you're young. With these fingers"—he fanned them under the amber lamping—"I might have been a master gem cutter."

"Instead of a pickpocket?"

"Such language," The Don said primly. "Such crudity."

Aura giggled and sipped at her drink.

"What I mean here is that you didn't necessarily set out to be the sexiest moll along this spit of sand. There were other ideas before that, posters on your walls. Ballerina. Movie star."

"Charlie's Angel," Aura said.

"Sure. A beauty with a gun. That's all I mean."

Peck called me over to scowl. "Never," he said. "Not in a trillion years."

But The Don showed no signs of letting up. He murmured along, rueful, humbled, refusing to examine her décolletage. And, as happened on those nights when the Don was on, Aura stayed with him, reeled in by his belief. There was no thought of the Romanians, not with Aura scooted to his side of the table, running her nail along his lifeline, leaning into his arm.

Until they appeared, the same two, stationed on each side of The Don, like ill angels. "If you'll excuse," The Don said. "These gentlemen appear to want a word."

I crouched in the doorway to the alley while the two of them shouted at The Don, who waved his delicate hands and fed them a series of whispered answers. This made me wonder if The Don knew Romanian, might even be Romanian, a fact he vaguely denied whenever Peck called him Gypsy Moth.

Whatever he said didn't sway his antagonists. One held and the other punched, a brisk blow over the left eye. The sound was awful, a soft buckling of flesh. Then one of them said: "Next time, the nose."

Off they went and in flew The Don, breathing heavily, waving me off, weaving through the dim back room and back to the table, where Aura sat in pretty confusion. "My apologies," he said. His cape dangled, sodden at the hem.

"*Oh!* Oh my gracious!" Aura stared at the blood trickling down the Don's cheek.

"Nothing," he said. He dabbed with a cocktail napkin. "Nothing."

"Are you in some kind of trouble?" Aura said.

"Don't be silly," The Don said. "You're being silly."

By the end of July he was staring backwards into his drinks. "Remember Lucinda Durban?" he'd say. "Remember Gloria Apodoca?"

Gloria Apodoca, Gloria with her buttery skin and coconut breath, her crisp bouffant and tapered waist. Gloria on a one-day layover from a million miles away, an heiress of Filipino extraction, pleasantly soused and dreaming dreams of simpler oceans. The Don wooed her with his every fiber, with everything he hoped to be and knew he wasn't, regaling her with his inadequacies, arguing against excessive drink, teasing out (then nestling into) her exorbitant loneliness. By one they were dancing a sweet, sloppy tango, The Don cooing into her ear, wearing her arms like a loose sweater, their feet drifting across the scabby pine until Peck grunted, switched off the lights, left the key on the bar.

The Don asked me if I remembered, and I remembered.

Gloria and everything besides, the sickly green stench of the pickled eggs next to the register, so like the reek of low tide that knifed in from the breakers as we were setting up, dusk flared across the gritty sand and slaps of light on the Atlantic, silvercaps of fallen sun, the soft rumble of surf, vendors under striped umbrellas, the aroma of hot dog and cinnamon bun sizzling out, kids dizzy from the Big Dipper and Tilt-a-Whirl, thumping along the walk in new pink skin, mothers pushing strollers in plump embarrassment, old couples bent like pigeons over crusts of gossip. I saw myself growing old in this place, a regular amid its cunning hopes. And The

Don was at the center of all that, a first and final hope of seduction. It never occurred to me that he might be on sabbatical from his own appointed end. He seemed to be making it up as he went along.

In the lone surviving photo of those months—an era my parents still refer to as "that unfortunate summer"—one views The Don in a crowd scene, along the route of some forgotten parade. His fingers are tweezing the billfold of the stout German in front of him. An expression of surprised mirth lights the lower half of his face: *Look what I found.*

As the mulch of August set in, departure haunted the awnings. The clientele sagged in prestige. The gift shops threw up sales. And The Don grew brazen. He howled over dull Pennsylvanians, pledged his love to teenage drink pimps from the Shore, spilled rum on a couple from Ithaca, staggering now in the glitter of unintended slapstick.

"A fool," Peck said. "A fool's fool."

I didn't argue, though something in his futility cheered me. He tried. He was still trying.

The second weekend in August, the Romanians appeared again and collared him in the middle of the bar. "Bashed his fucking head," Peck said. "With a fucking, like, one of those walking sticks, those carved numbers with a silver tip. He went down like potatoes, this girl he's working going off like a siren and the Romas screaming *gumbah* this and *gumbah* that." Peck shook his rag. "I called the pigs and you know what that crazy fucking thief does? Splits out the back door."

I couldn't help feeling that my absence had allowed this. I would have been able to protect The Don, I was sure, to screen the Romas long enough for him to escape. It would have been a thrilling, dangerous thing, a chase down the purring neon, the knobbled wood.

Instead, I'd been up in Connecticut, skulking around my parents' house, swinging my father's golf clubs sort of close to lamps, fishing Merits from my mom's purse. I fantasized about upending the dinner table, or slipping my father's wallet from the back pocket of his trousers. But nothing ever happened. I passed the lamb, he passed the peas. We conducted our small transactions under a cloud of disappointment.

"No lie," Peck told me. "He better get right with those psychos. I will not have this kind of shit ruining our good name."

When The Don appeared the next night, the regulars shook their heads and moved away. But this was his place. This was where he came, where his public self resided, and even Peck, burrowed in his loamy hate, even Peck understood this.

"You okay?" I said.

The Don had arranged his bandage like a beret, though it had bled through a bit. "Listen up. Yonder sits my Minerva alone, you see? A G&T girl, dollars to donuts. When she gets oiled up, even her snatch smells like gin. Deliver this drink, Pancho, with my compliments. Don't give me that look. Excessive responsibility will ruin the lines of your face. Go." He held the drink out.

"Amazing," Peck said, watching him depart. "Disgusting. Those Romas are going to bust his head like a melon."

Only it wasn't the Romas who got him. Not the ones we expected, anyway.

Labor Day weekend came at last, and steam rose from the water at dawn, a chill rolling in on the salty back of night, signaling the end of summer. The Don had spent the previous week in jail, having plucked a gold locket from a friend of a friend of a local deputy, then made matters worse by fencing into the hands of the new district narc. He'd gotten greedy as he sensed the tourists drifting away, back to their staplers and particle board. During the year, Peck said, The Don worked as a hotel clerk.

So on this Sunday he was restless for a taste, a last fresh face, restless even after he settled in with a young summer waitress, washed-out, muddy-eyed, full of talk about her departure, bored and boring and easy. The Don jolted her drinks with nips from the flasks that lined his cape in velvet loops. He made no indication of noticing when the second girl—the little Romanian, that is—settled into the doorway.

She was very real in her grief and even slightly beautiful without her hat. A thin glow rose from her shoulders. The hair braided down her back swayed like black rope.

The Don ignored her. Determinedly, at great expense to his élan, he ignored her. The other patrons, the regulars even, those serious about the business of killing themselves with drink, began to look upon her with pity. Part of it was how cold she looked, in just her white gown. You wanted to throw a shawl on her.

"Pregnant as diapers," Peck scoffed. "Look at that gut. What did I tell you?" Peck had been telling me this for some weeks, though I had chosen not to believe him, attributing his speculation to envy. Now there was no denying: the swell of her belly shone under the streetlamp. Her eyes were somber and she looked steadily at The Don, from ten feet away.

"Do you, like, know that girl?" the waitress said finally.

"Nonsense," The Don said. "You're the girl I know."

"I think you better settle this, Romeo," said the waitress.

The Don seized her hand and in this seizure his composure

dissolved. He swiveled around and drew his lips back, as if to growl at the little Romanian, and she stepped away from the light, looking terribly young and sad and unsurprised in her sadness.

I had seen, over the three months of our acquaintance, The Don perform a number of disreputable actions, had even assisted him in lesser transgressions. But I'm not sure I'd seen him do anything dishonorable. This action, I mean, struck me immediately as a betrayal.

The waitress, to her credit, shoved off.

Now The Don did a quick sweep of the bar, his glance settling on me for a moment—not even a moment, a flickering—before he looked away and moved to the door and spoke to the girl in low hurried tones. We could see them in the halo of the storefront, him looming over her, all shrugs and footwork, running his line, her nodding, seeming to want to lean against him.

The Don looked up and saw us, our panting tongues and red eyeballs. He scuttled her away, down the sidewalk.

"The last of the red-hot lovers," Scoonie said.

"Maybe the Romas put her up to it," I said.

"Damn straight they put her up to it," Peck said. "Those guys are her brothers, you little fucknut. They're *family*." Peck tapped his wedding band on a faux brass accent. He had a wife and a fat little kid stashed away somewhere. He'd shown me the photos one time. "I gotta get out of this place," Peck said. "I gotta grow the fuck up."

We figured The Don might go AWOL after this business with the girl, but a few hours later he was back. I was alone, stacking chairs, running water for the mop. Peck had recently granted me the duties of closing: dumping garbage in the bacterial Dumpster, fingering wet butts from the drink drains, dragging the gray mop across the gray floor. This was authority.

The Don hovered out front in his cape, like a tattered raven. I wondered how long he'd been there. "Let's do a nightcap," he said. "A whiskey. Neat." He showed me his teeth; I couldn't tell if he was grinning or wincing.

"I've got to close," I told him.

"Don't be, you're being silly." He pushed past me. "Come on, Panch."

"Seriously," I said. "Peck's counting on me."

He cocked his head. "You really take this stuff serious, don't you?"

"What stuff?"

"The whole routine. Okay. You work. I can wait."

I took a few swipes with the mop and listened to him hum one of his melancholy songs, a song like you might hear at the end of an opera, after the big deathbed scene. I laid the mop against the counter. "What happened with that girl?" I said.

The Don shook his head. "Can't a man get a drink around here? Is that still possible? Come on, now. I'm buying."

I set out a tumbler for him. Peck would have made him lay his money down, kept him honest. But I didn't have that kind of heart. And, the truth is, though I felt a great anger toward The Don, I also felt flattered. He was here, after all. I imagined he'd run from somewhere far away to seek my counsel.

I poured him his whiskey, neat, and The Don took a gulp. "What it is," he said. "People try to hem you in, okay? That's a lot of what life is about, that process. A guy like me, let's face it: I'm not the best-looking guy. I got the Potapenko complexion, brown as old onions, these ratty eyes. And my earnings capacity, I mean, I'm not about to franchise. But these are just things to overcome, okay? Because when I'm on my game, when I'm on, Pancho, they don't stand a chance. I see a woman and love her so purely, the motions of her face and her body, that shyness and that bravery underneath, the length of her calf, that flesh where tit meets rib. And that love, it's like a kind of leverage. When I start to love a woman, in that first second or two, instantly I mean, I become what I want to be. I amaze myself." The Don smiled. Loose skin bracketed his mouth.

"Sure," I said.

Outside, a drizzle had started in, and the gulls shrieked. The Don slapped at the plastic banner over the bar, a buy-one-get-one-free Labor Day humdinger. He was back to looking debonair, dragging his fingers through his hair. "You never know who's watching," he said. And it was true. You never *did* know. When The Don was on, when he was humming, when even the chintzy lights of the strip agreed to illuminate him, there was always somebody watching, some girl, some possibility. It was only a matter of recognizing this possibility and seizing it. That's what I wanted: to be a part of the play; to be, someday, the star.

"What are you going to do, Pancho?" The Don said.

"I'm going to stay. Peck says they'll give me a shot at bartender before long."

"Peck says." The Don snorted softly. "How old are you?"

"Almost twenty."

"So what—you're going to make a life in the alcoholic arts?"

I had not, to this point, conceived of my life as a totality, a thing, a process that, in the long term, might be determined by short-term decisions.

"For now," I told him. "You're the one who said it; about being who you want and all. My folks, this whole plan they have for me. It's not real. It's phony." I took a swig of whiskey and swallowed a cough.

"Don't be a dumbass," The Don said sharply. "Those are your people. That's where you come from."

"It's not where I have to end up."

The Don squinted. "Make your own way in the world, that it?"

"Why shouldn't I make my own way in the world? Shit. Isn't that what you're doing? One day at a time. Find what you love. Don't I have the right to do that?" It was his look that bothered me, as if *I* was the fool, as if I were the one screwing up.

"Okay, Pancho. Settle down."

I rose to my full height and looked down on the The Don, his lousy fading widow's peak. "Don't tell me to settle down. Fuck. You sound like my fucking dad." The Don said nothing. He stared into his drink. "Say something," I said. "Say one fucking thing. Jesus. What a phony. You're the one who got that girl pregnant. You're the one who, who should be thinking about his responsibilities. I'm still young. I can dream whatever I want."

The Don was quiet now. He reached across the bar and poured himself another; the whiskey rippled under the lights. He took a sip and stared at me for a long moment and I still loved him in that moment, though I didn't want to.

"It's one thing to have dreams," he said slowly. "And another to chase them down. Listen to me, Pancho. I know some things. Go back to where you belong." The play had gone out of his voice. There was something even hard there, a kind of contempt I'd not heard before.

I wasn't crying exactly but my breathing was wet and my throat hurt. I tried to make a funny face, like he was just a clown yakking away. But The Don held his stare. "You ever been in this place in February? Have you, Pancho? It's like a fucking morgue, okay? Not a movie set. A fucking morgue. Where the dead stay. You hear me?"

I took another sip, to dull my throat. "What happened with that girl?" I said. "Peck says you knocked her up."

The Don looked away. "*Knocked her up.* Some bartender you'll make. Is that the kind of language your parents taught you? Is it?"

"What happened?"

"It's a complex situation," he said softly.

"What's so complex? Is she pregnant or not?"

The Don's jaw clenched and unclenched. "Oh for Chrissake!" he snarled. "What business is this of yours, anyway? You're not my father, or my fucking kid. You're just some rich brat slumming for a summer. What gives you the right?" He looked off toward the ocean, as if waiting for something to transpire above the black waves.

I could see now that The Don wanted me out of his life; wanted an escape from the expectations I heaped upon him. "Listen," he said finally, "you're my main man, okay? You're my guy, Pancho. If I'd gotten that girl—Jesus—don't you think I'd tell you? You're the first guy I'd tell. You listen to me, all right? I know some things." He drained his drink and smiled. "Let's just lock this dump up, okay?"

I began frisking my pockets for the keys. "Shit," I said. I looked down the bar, checked beside the register, twice, and all along the sideboards. I rooted around behind the bar on my hands and knees. My first week closing solo and I'd managed to fuck up.

Somewhere above me I could hear The Don's laughter, sawing away. "Looking for these?" he said. From his cape he drew my key ring, chunky with dutiful silver, and swirled the loop around his fingers, one to the next, like a gymnast on the rings.

"Thanks, asshole," I said. Outside the sky spattered on, the hotels shuttered, the strip shut down, drained of its spruce, the amusement park a failing endeavor already, the arms and legs of the rides frozen in the dark. Past the piers, the lighthouse stood on a bluff, facing the ocean like a prop.

"You should go home," The Don said. He hesitated a moment, then tossed me the keys and took up the whiskey bottle. With great care, he filled his flasks and placed them in their velvet belt loops. Then he picked up his tumbler and hurled it at the pickled-egg jar, missing badly. "I've always hated those things," he said. "They stink like the ocean," he said. "I'll sweep that up. Sorry."

We heard a lot of things about The Don later. That he'd been killed by the Romas, his skull dashed on the breakers. That he'd been forced to marry the girl, held at gunpoint during the ceremony, and moved with her to Cleveland. That he'd nicked a diamond from Big Marek, one of the Russians, and wound up in Sing Sing.

This was the apocrypha of Don Viktor, stories told to fill the long pauses of autumn. However it went, he knew the time had come for him to return to who he was. It took me a bit longer, plunging, as I was, through youth's dizzy cycles of ignorance and want. Who could have known, then, that I couldn't be anything I imagined?

Years later, the casinos would go up and light the walk forever, blinding everything. The papers still carry items from time to time about some lost gull crashing into a marquee. Every night, the place draws slot zombies and card counters by the thousands, the amateur escape artists of our age, garish and hope-drunk, as if the fairy-tale kiss of fate might change their lives forever.

I was only beginning to understand fairy tales on the night The Don hurled his glass and flew off. I was still mesmerized by his belief, by the myth of reinvention, as were his women, his many women, though fewer, probably, than in my memory. With The Don, when he returns to me now, he is always in that seaside bar: the warm summer fog and the smell of lemon rinds and gin and the lights soft upon closing and Gloria Apodoca folded into his cape, her lips red along his neck as they dance their last slow tango. In this version of my life, The Don looks up drowsily, winks, winks at *me*, a sweet bird of beauty winging new toward love.

Run Away, My Pale Love

This was just before my thirtieth birthday. I was in graduate school, of all places. I had no idea why. None of us did. We were extremely well spoken rubber duckies. You could push us in any one direction and we would flounder on forever. Sometimes, in the drowsy winter hallways, my conscience would rear up and remind me I was dumb with luck. Other times, I wished they'd turn the whole place into a homeless shelter.

But the day I'm talking about was early spring. The callery pears were in blossom, thousands of tiny white camisoles. I was out in front of the Comp Lit compound with Legget, watching the undergrads. We were vaguely aware of the distinctions between them. Mostly, they were tan calves drifting past.

A woman entered my field of vision from the right. She had the plumpest cheeks I'd ever seen. Her eyes were pinched at the corners, and blue patches stood out below them. She looked as if she hadn't slept in a year. Every other woman I could think of seemed stingy and coarse and obvious by comparison. She waved timidly at Legget.

"You like that, do you?" he said.

"Who is she?"

"She's in my French class." Legget stubbed out his cigarette. "Polish, I think."

"What's her name?"

"Don't know," Legget said. "She doesn't say much."

For the next week, I walked around babbling about The Polish Woman. "You know me," I said. "I don't gawk. I'm not a gawker." This was more or less true. Somewhere in the mid-twenties it dawned on me that female beauty didn't require any encouragement from me. Female beauty was doing just fine on its own. But I couldn't get this woman out of my head.

Legget diagnosed sexual infatuation.

"Can't I just have an aesthetic experience?" I said. "Like spotting a rare species, a species you might see once and never again, for the rest of your life?"

"Spare me," Legget said.

Two months later, in the computer lab, a woman in a white blouse swept into the seat next to mine. "Is it all right?" she said. Her accent was excruciating: the burred diphthongs of Russian, the sulky lilt of French. My heart did a little arpeggio.

"You're Polish," I said.

She turned and there was her face again. Her lips drew together, as if stung by some impending calamity. "Yah. How do you know?"

I explained about Legget. She nodded slowly.

"Do you like Kosinski?" I said.

"Oh yah!" she said. "Have you read *Painted Bird*?"

"Sure," I said. "Wow. It's hard to find anyone who's read Kosinski." This was true. I myself, for instance, had not read Kosinski, though I'd heard he was quite good. "What a writer!" I said. "What sentences!" On and on I went until, finally, at a loss for what to say next, I asked for her phone number.

She looked at me for a few seconds—I was in my teaching uniform, a rumpled white button-down and khakis—then wrote her name on a piece of paper: *Basha.*

"I don't do this normally," I said. "But, I mean, I really love Kosinski."

And then she was standing on the median of Summit Avenue, lit up inside a beige windbreaker. She looked elegant and chimerical: the head of a lioness, the body of a swan. At dinner I choked on my chicken korma. That was just for starters. I got lost on the way to the theater. I misplaced my wallet, and had to race home to get cash. We were twenty minutes late to the movie—a British drawing-room melodrama—and sat in the darkened theater trying to figure out who was doomed and who fated. I spent most of the time smelling Basha, glancing at her profile, my fingers greasy with popcorn.

The amateur psychologists in the crowd will perhaps sense the significance of the lost wallet: *The subject subconsciously enacts a fantasy in which he is stripped of his identity through a powerful, exotic love.*

To which I would respond: *Doy hickey.*

I was ravenous for a love so grandiose as to obliterate my life. Most every relationship I'd formed in the past five years had gone south: romantic entanglements, friendships, professional alliances. One friend referred to me as a train wreck. Another suggested "emotional atom bomb" as perhaps closer to the mark. The ones I couldn't scare away, I managed to drive off over some perceived slight. I was the world's welterweight champion of the silent feud. I didn't see it that way, of course. People just kept letting me down. It never occurred to me that I sought out rejection, engineered the drama of fresh grievances to distract me from older, stale forms of grief.

But that's not the story I'm telling now. No one—except those paid to listen—really wants to hear your musty songs of self-contempt. What we want is the glib aria of disastrous love, which is, finally, the purest expression of self-contempt.

Her full name was Basha Sabina Olszewska. She pronounced her last name beautifully: Olshevska. It meant something like a birch tree, she said. I thought of Frost: the pale trunk, the quick fire. She came from Katowice, an industrial city in the west of Poland. She hoped to become a translator. English was her fifth language.

She had a sense of humor as well. Imagine. She told me a story about dining with the Dean of Students at a welcoming banquet for exchange students. "They brought him steak," she said. "I couldn't believe the size, David. It was like a car tire. Everyone was quiet for a second and just at that minute I turned to him and said: 'You have such a huge meat!'"

This story thrilled me, its slapstick reference to the male part. Basha knew what a cock was! She understood the great harmless joke that all cocks come to in the end. And this idea, however improbably, led to the idea that she might touch my cock.

We were eating at my place. She was sitting there at my table, daintily cutting her chicken. I told stories about my life that suggested—far less subtly than I supposed—what a terrific guy I was. I cleared her plate and took it to the sink. Wasn't I the disarmingly liberated bachelor type? She stood. I stepped in front of her and let my face fall forward. She executed a brisk little sidestep. My lips smeared the side of her cheek. A pinecone fell from the tree out-side, striking the roof with a soft thud, as if to close the subject.

Later, standing outside her dorm, I said: "Will I ever get to kiss you?"

Her lips pursed, like a waiter who is out of the most popular item on the menu. The light fell across her in frets. "Such an Ameri-can question!" She told me about some Finnish jerk she'd fallen for first term. And now she was returning to Poland and felt too vul-nerable—the word seemed to swirl around her tongue—to get involved.

To which I wanted to say: involved? Who needs *involved*?

This was one of the advantages of age. I'd been rejected enough times to understand that prudence meant little in the face of sus-tained negotiation. Virtue was a better guide, all things considered. You could maybe depend on virtue. But a guy like me, with my wonderful rage, my American case of Manifest Destiny, I wasn't about to back down from a little prudence. "Sure," I said. "I under-stand. I hope we can still be friends."

Basha was so relieved at my grace, she gave herself to me. She needed the help of a large bottle of inexpensive sauvignon blanc, which disappeared down her throat, cup by cup, while I watched in cau-tious rapture. It seemed terribly important that I do nothing to startle her. Slowly, perceptibly, my kitchen grew warm with the promise of contact. I can't recall a word that passed between us. There was only the wine, my silence, her mouth fixing to the rim of her cup, the slight, glottal pull of her underlip against and away from its surface, her white throat reaching up, descending.

We kissed and she smiled, her lips turning back on themselves. Her teeth were faintly discolored, as if she'd had a quick bite of ashes. I had never seen the classic Slavic facial structure at such close quarters. When she laughed her cheeks rose with the strange, graceful bulk of glaciers and her eyes became Mongol slashes. Frowning, her face took on the milky petulance of a Tartar princess. Even at rest, impassive, her face expressed the severe emotions I associated with true love, which I had always known to be exquisite and doomed and slightly stylized.

I felt the pleasing thickness of her, damp beneath her garments. We were on my mattress, yanking off clothes. She had narrow shoulders, tiny budded breasts. Her arms and belly were robed in baby fat.

We made love, or fucked, did that thing where our center parts fit and unfit, a half dozen times, in panicky sessions, ten minutes or so, until she cried out *tak! tak!* then fell still. She consented to my movements with her body and spoke only once, toward dawn, saying, as my hand brushed up her thigh, "I am having so wet." I knew then—at that exact moment—Basha had been sent to rescue me from the dull plight of my life.

This, it would turn out, is the main thing we had in common: a susceptibility to the brassy escapism of myth.

I saw her across the street, her arms poking out of a red dress with white polka dots, the fabric tight around her bum. She came to me and kissed me and I could smell the rot of her mouth. And the rot of her mouth turned me on! (Is there nothing the early days of love won't fetishize?)

We went to the mall to buy last-minute gifts. Basha circled the pavilion, fretting over a belt, a bottle of lotion, blushing at the inquiries of the sales staff. She was a nervous shopper, which I took to be a mark of her unfamiliarity with the ritual. I had all sorts of crappy ideas rattling around my head about life in Poland. I knew, vaguely, that the Poles had broken from the Soviet Bloc. But I still imagined a lumpen gulag: endless lines, bare shelves, faces like potatoes in kerchiefs. And my poor Basha trapped amid this needy vulgarity! I stood behind her and called out to the clerks: *One of those! Make it two! Why not? Do you have this in black?*

Our relationship was filed under *dalliance*, which allowed us to write one another without much pressure. Basha was an excellent correspondent. She made it a point to send me sexy photos of herself. My favorite showed her leaning toward the camera, kissing at a cigarette, mascara smeared, hair tousled—a Bond girl at the end of a long vodka party.

That summer I got stoned, sat on my porch, tried to figure out where everyone had gone. Across the street, guys with whistles were running a girl's soccer camp, which I could watch if I wasn't too obvious. The girls were sweet and clumsy. They lacked the essentials of the sport—the ability to steal and confront and tackle—but their legs enjoyed flirting with these ideas. I was supposed to be writing a dissertation.

My answering machine was the enemy. Often, returning from the grocery store, or the Greek diner where I took suppers, I gazed at the red zero flashing smugly and punched the machine. Then, one day, there was a message.

Hayizmeimeezyucullme.

When I called her back, Basha wanted to know, immediately, if she would ever see me again. "I made a breakup with my boyfriend," she said.

"What boyfriend?"

"It doesn't matter," she said. "I have my vacations at end of August."

At the airport in Warsaw she came running, her eyes blurry hazel, a skirt shaping her hips, and she was far too beautiful for me, my sharp face and chickeny bones. I felt (as I often feel) a dramatic error in the accounting, though she pressed herself to me and made me feel, thereby, in the midst of that lousy airport, with its plastic counters and vague feculence, different from myself, heroic.

We found a cheap hotel and signed in as man and wife. Basha did the talking, while the concierge squinted at her.

"She thinks I am a whore," Basha said in the elevator. She smiled, her gums like a second, wetter smile. "Maybe I am a whore." She shut the door to our room, and tore the button off my pants. I'd seen this sort of thing, in films hoping to suggest reckless passion. But this was the first time I'd been inside the animal experience, so famished for physical love as to overleap the gooey crescendo of intimacy. We never even got our shirts off.

Basha wanted nothing to do with clitoral stimulation, tricky positioning, langorous gazes. Put it in, was her agenda. Let the flesh speak. Her face went rubbery. She took on the aspect of a madwoman plucked from one of Hogarth's Bedlam prints, ready to tear her hair, throw shit, which pleased me, as did her internal muscles, which yielded in rings of contraction. Sun from the window lit a glaze of perspiration on her small white breasts. Her hips rocked.

"Make big come," she said. "Make big come in my pussy."

"Tell me—"

"Now. Now-now-*now*."

Afterward, her body looked like something tossed ashore.

Basha reached down and took hold of me: "You have huge meat."

I laughed.

"Really," she said.

"I'm pretty sure I have normal meat," I said.

"No," she said. "I remember the first time we were together, when I first saw, thinking this."

I studied her expression for some sign of caginess. But caginess was not her style. She didn't speak about the particulars of sex in the same way an American woman might. And she appeared quite serious in her assessment, as if my size were a matter she had considered privately.

My ego flew in wild circles overhead. Is there nothing man desires more than to be regaled about his own huge meat?

Basha didn't remember her father, who had died when she was two years old. He was no more than a blurry figure in photographs, with her tiny arrow of a nose. Her first love—her only great love, from what I could tell—was her stepfather Tomas, a gentle mathematician who had worshiped Basha's mother.

"What happened to him?" I said.

"He died when I was eight," she said. "Returning from a conference in Germany. There was snow on the road."

"My God," I said. "I'm so sorry."

I reached for Basha, but she slipped to the side of the bed and sat up, regarding me curiously. "Don't be sorry. I barely remember."

In Kraków we went to see the palace, but it was closed for repairs, so we walked to the other end of the plaza. The tourist bureau had organized a folk dancing festival, surly teenagers spinning in peasant garb. Basha herself wore a summer dress, loose around the legs, and open-toed sandals. I thought about all the girls in their summer dresses, and tried to understand why I cared only to look at Basha.

We made love in our muggy pension room, lathered one another in the shower, then returned to the plaza, to feel the breeze on our limbs, which were sore in secret places, to watch the stars against the drape of night, and browse the stalls of painted eggs and cigarette cases. The cafes were open, the tabletops lit by bouncing candles.

My own tranquility astounded me.

"What do you think about?" Basha said.

"Night," I said. "A beautiful night like this."

She squeezed my hand and leaned in for a kiss. Her eyes were deep green and perfectly serious. In a soft, almost embarrassed voice, she said: "I want to come to America to make a life with you, David." Her hands were trembling. Her breathing was ragged. This was all terribly real. I had to remind myself.

"Yes?" she whispered. "What do you think about it?"

Hadn't I come to Poland in the hopes of just such a plea? Don't we all, in the private kingdom of our desires, dream about such pleas?

And yet there was something deflating about the declaration. Without warning, in one sentence, Basha had called an end to the hunt, laid herself before me, forced me to make good on the promises of my extravagant furious charm. I felt my heart chop.

We were ideally suited to the long-distance relationship, with its twisted calculus of wish fantasy and deprivation. We wrote long epistles full of desire and ardent grief. We perfected the art of nostalgia: extracting the finer moments from the tangle of actual experience, burnishing them with new longing. We took the inconvenience of our love as proof of its profundity.

And so, Christmas in Poland. Katowice struck me as suitably impoverished. Men selling carp on the corners, slashing the fish until blood soaked their aprons, while the wives peddled roe. Everyone looked glum and underdressed; the sidewalks ran off into mud.

Basha lived with her mother, but they were both at work. She'd left me the key to the apartment. Her building was part of a massive Soviet-style *panelak*, crinkled like a fan, five stories of concrete smeared with soot, stairwells sharp with piss. Her room was the size of a cell: a single bed, a dresser, a desk with my letters neatly stacked in one corner. Over the bed she'd taped a picture of us kissing on a street corner in Kraków. I'd taken the photo myself, holding the camera with one hand while hauling her into an embrace. The white pelt of Basha's cheek was draped across the frame, her eyes closed, her mouth thrown toward the kiss. The photo was blurred: as if the action captured had been terribly swift, or the moment dreamed.

Outside, snow fell like confetti, dissolving on the pavement. Every time I heard the tock of a woman's shoes my body tensed.

Basha burst into the apartment finally, out of breath, her eyes glassy. I experienced the brief paralysis of gratification. *You mean this is actually mine?* Her hands slipped beneath my sweater. Her minty tongue touched mine. Basha backed me into her room. The smell of her rose up, a sweet bacterial tang. She let out a luxurious sigh as I slid into her. Such drama! It was like leaping onto Broadway cock-first.

And later, scrubbed and pink-eared, I sat at the Olszewska's dining-room table, gorged on rice laced with cumin and slivers of sautéed liver. Mamu appeared, flushed from the cold (and, it would turn out, a good deal of wine). She was a handsome woman, wide cheeks and a plucked mouth. Basha's face bloomed. It was clear at once that they were deeply in love, as mothers and daughters sometimes grow to be, without the interfering needs of men.

I stood and Mamu looked me over. I could see Basha watching us, the slowing of her breath. Mamu shook my hand and announced, in her wobbly English, that she was delighted to meet me. Then she pulled me into a sloppy hug and Basha laughed and pulled me back to her side, scolding Mamu in Polish, a language that seemed to me always, in the mouths of the Olszewska women, a volley of quick and playful whispers.

What did I have to do? Stand there and look pretty. This was the secret dividend of loving a woman from a foreign country: very little was required of me.

"We will have wodka," Mamu said.

"*Vodka*," Basha said.

"*Vodka,*" Mamu corrected herself elaborately.

Yes! Vodka with bitter tonic and lemon wedges, drunk from tall glasses. And later, in Mamu's room, plum brandy from snifters. The three of us were huddled at the foot of her bed; there was no other place to sit. Her room accommodated a single bed, a book-shelf, a small dresser for clothes.

Mamu was one of those smokers whose motions are so calm and practiced, so assumed, that the act becomes an extension of their personality. She preferred a brand called Petit Ceours, whose box was decorated in tiny gray hearts. The cigarettes themselves were as slender as lollipop sticks. Mamu could kill one in six drags, though often she let them burn down untended, the ashes making elegant snakes. She seemed to enjoy the option of smoking as much as the act.

Basha and I took the tram to the central plaza, with its smooth new cobblestone and stately, gabled buildings, refurbished with foreign money and painted in cake-frosting colors. These housed clubs and restaurants and clothing shops, for tourists of course, but also for the new class of strivers represented by Basha and her friends, who had learned the first lesson of the bourgeoisie: that the acquisition of wealth required, to some mysterious degree, the appearance of wealth.

We visited a few clubs, smoky places full of old pop songs and young people trying hard to acquire the defensive irony of American culture. This made me sad. But liquor helped soften my sadness, helped me occupy a little more gracefully my role as Basha's exuberant Americanski. We wound up in some hotel lounge. Basha was there, next to me, laughing. The other women, dour and beautiful, watched me. I downed shot after shot and proposed toasts in mangled French and serenaded Basha with a fair rendition of Elvis Presley. Some fellow pulled a glass pipe from his pocket. "Hash," he said. "Hashish." I smoked some of that, too. Sure. I was the star. The star drinks. The star smokes.

Then we were outside, on the stumbling cobblestone, under the splotchy moon. Basha folded herself into me. Everything about her seemed perfect just then: her cheeks, the way her mouth smooshed vowels, her new decadence, her pale body. She was emotionally inobvious. That was true. But wasn't that just part of the mystery? Wasn't that, in some sense, the entire point?

That we made love I recognized only by the feeling of my lower body, a wet, suctiony joy. Most nights I would have curled around her, kissing the skin between her shoulder blades, my low arm going slowly numb beneath her. But the bed didn't seem entirely solid, seemed more in the nature of an ocean. Salt rose in my throat and I staggered to the bathroom. My body heaved and gasped. I suspected—as do all unpracticed drinkers—that I would never feel right again. Far above, I could see the racks of emollients, Basha's cherished blow-dryer, panty hose laid like molted skin across the radiator, a calliope of homely bras.

There was a tap on the door. Basha. Basha come to rescue her lover.

I struggled to my feet and opened the door. Mamu stood in her robe, blinking. I was naked. My penis dangled. The sweetness of her daughter's sex, like flesh that has been perfumed and licked, rose into the air between us. I wanted to duck behind the door, but in that moment such an action seemed to constitute an accusation.

"You are sick?" Mamu said. She was careful not to let her gaze drop below my chest.

"I drank too much," I said. "Wodka." I pantomimed taking a shot, and in this motion, as my arm rose to my mouth, my fingers flipped toward my lips, I became acutely aware of my cock, rising up, settling back.

"You would like tea?" Mamu said.

"Oh no." I laid a palm on my stomach. Mamu glanced down, not entirely understanding the gesture, and her eyes settled there for a moment, not even a moment, a charged little half moment.

How long had it been since Mamu had looked upon the chicken-necked vanity of a man's sex? She had buried two husbands, and, by Basha's account, no longer considered the idea. But Basha did not yet understand what a stubborn customer the body is. The heart may turn the lights out. The body never closes for business.

"No tea?" she said.

"No, thank you."

"Okay," Mamu whispered. She stepped back into the hallway and turned; her robe traced the soft square of her hips. She had the same body as Basha, after all, only dragged by time, by the tolls of motherhood.

"Sorry for waking you up," I said.

She turned back to me, and her face emerged from the shadows so abruptly it was as if she had leapt toward me. I ducked behind the door. This was not a conscious act. My body, drunken and shy, simply reacted. And yet the expression that settled onto Mamu's face then seemed unutterably sad. Her teeth carved out a tiny failed smile. "It doesn't matter to me," she said.

*   *   *

Mamu spent the day before my departure preparing borscht. The windows fogged with a bouquet of onions fried in chicken fat, celery, carrots, peppers, the subtle acrid undercurrent of beets. I'd never eaten borscht. That was the joke. From time to time, I shambled to the kitchen to fetch tea from the porcelain kettle that stood, perpetually steeping, on the narrow ledge between oven and sink. I paused to watch Mamu core the eyes out of a potato.

"She is sad," Mamu said quietly. "Are you sad?"

"Yes," I said.

She raised her hands, as if to make a gesture, and her fingertips came to rest on my cheekbone. I could smell the dirt and onions on her hands, which were beautiful, pink and swollen, the backs laced with delicate veins. "Yes. Sad."

After dinner we drank vodka. Mamu put some folk music on the record player, and Basha attempted to teach me the rudiments of a polka. Then Mamu rose from her seat, handed me her softer body, which moved with a surprising buoyancy.

And later, piled into her room, Mamu pulled a silver punch bowl from beneath her bed, filled with family photos. There she was, thirty years ago, on a youth-brigade outing, a pretty, stylish teenager in a uniform and a beret. She looked at me as I looked at the photos, leaned against my shoulder. Her face sang out the same caption again and again: *This is me, young and beautiful!*

There were other photos she wanted me to see: Basha looking darling in a white pinafore, nestled on the lap of her stepfather, fending off sleep with a gummy smile. Mamu set her hand on my thigh. She leaned toward me. For a moment I thought she would kiss me, that her red, smoky mouth would seek mine. But I was missing it. The person she was reaching for was Basha. The photos fell from her lap, her youth, her motherhood, her daughter, the men she loved, all tumbling onto the rug, faceup, facedown, the bowl used for storing them showing streaks of tarnish under the amber light.

Basha clambered off the bed and went down onto her forearms, pushing her backside into the air. She was quite drunk.

"Do you like the way I look like this?"

It took me a moment to gather my voice and Basha laughed, as we should wish all women to laugh, at the fallacy of their depravity, at the idea that anything, in the end, can disgust them. "I want anal love," she said, making the word sound French and exquisite.

Is it cruel for me to repeat her words like this? Should I lie, make them somehow prettier, more poetic? But this is what she said. This is the form her desire took at that moment. Or perhaps, less flatteringly, she intuited my need for a memorable degradation, some form of going-away present.

"Are you sure?" I said.

"Put some jelly." Basha sucked in a little breath and pushed back. The heel of her palms pressed down and her arms tensed. I braced my heel against the radiator. The knuckles of her spine buckled softly. Her face was pressed to the rug and her eyes were closed and she was smiling.

I could hear Mamu in the bathroom, making her ablutions before bed.

"We should stop," I said.

Basha shook her head: *No, it feels good, but it hurts, let's keep trying.*

There were other women around, more suitable, in baggy sweaters and glasses much like mine, their clocks fizzing away. But I was in no shape to cooperate with them. The last thing I wanted was a woman who actually understood me. Once back in the States, that is, face to face with the prospect of a reasonable adulthood, I fell back under the aegis of my own bloated heroism. I knew I was being played. But that, too, is a part of love. I missed Basha. I missed her Old World manners, which made me feel debonair. I missed Mamu's greasy borscht and her confused longing. I missed their warm little apartment, where I was always the center of attention.

Katowice was made new by May. The buildings, ash-streaked and rotten in winter, bloomed with mongrel hyacinth. Sun baked the mud to dirt. Shirts fluttered brightly on laundry lines and kids kicked soccer balls in the courtyards and couples in long shadows strolled the plaza at dusk. With the windows thrown open, the breeze carried the fragrance of broiled chicken and baked sesame seeds, the sweet reek of garbage.

And the women! The women of Katowice unpeeled themselves, plum-titted, translucent, with cheeks a mile square and big sleepy asses, teenagers in sullen halter tops, business molls slotted into rayon suits, college students spilling from green miniskirts, young mommies pushing strollers. And the girls of the meat shops, whose flanks and chops sweat in glass cases, whose beauty hid beneath tiers of acne, who handled the sweet, smoky kielbasa as if handling thick lovers—brisk, worldly imitations of sex!

Each morning Basha and Mamu bustled off to work while I got up and pretended to write. I was hard at work on what was—to my knowledge—the longest outline in academic history; 471 pages, not counting footnotes. At noon I fixed myself a breakfast of eggs, sugar-cured bacon, rolls pan-fried in the fat. Then I settled down for a nap, listening to the yips of the kids on the playground below. It was all quite bohemian. I smoked Walet cigarettes, at 85 groszy a pack, which tasted of cloves and dung.

In the evenings I talked literature with Mamu. She'd studied philology at the university, and devoured the Western Canon. *Die Blechtrummel* was an after-dinner mint to her. I bounced a few of my ideas her way and they came back deboned and neatly skinned. Basha preferred TV, which consisted, in large part, of American sitcoms dubbed into Polish by a single droning monotone.

Aside from sexual congress, during which her mind and body seemed open to the fluctuations of experience, she remained determinedly opaque. She was not dumb, or shallow. She had mastered five languages and spoke each of them beautifully. There seemed no sound her tongue couldn't make. She simply mistrusted the depth of her feelings.

But even our glorious sex life wilted under the rigor of permanence. Basha kept me on what the behaviorialists would recognize as a variable reinforcement schedule. She wanted to be cuddled, fawned over, stroked like a child. If I pushed for more, she claimed to be sore, or tired. I couldn't figure this out. Where had the wanton accomplice of our early days gone? Once a week or so I staged a blowout, on some despicable pretext, so as to storm out of the apartment, valiant and misunderstood, and wander the weedy banks of the Valia river, whose slick tides were the color of veinous blood; so as to return to the balm of her negligent love, which was for me like floating in a warm sea.

*　*　*

Toward the end of July an old professor, who had known me in a steadier time, tracked me down. He needed a lecturer for fall. The job itself was no great shakes. But his intention was clear. He was offering me reentry. A decent paycheck. Enough respect to take another pass at my dissertation. "What are you doing over there anyway?" he said.

Basha remained unconvinced. "You won't leave," she said. "You love me too much." She refused to imagine that I had another life, beyond her beauty, thick with the troubled symptoms of adulthood.

"You can come to the States," I said. "Like we talked about."

For all her brave claims of a year ago, Basha said nothing about this plan. Instead, we let the weeks drift by, watched the dour sun elongate the days. The cedars shed elegant white scrolls along the aimless paths where we went to eat ice cream.

On the eve of my departure I took Basha to Katowice's toniest bistro. We ordered coq au vin and tenderloin braised in anisette. I had hoped to take a last walk on the plaza, but by the end of the meal Basha's complexion looked like cement. She barely touched her food. Back at home, Mamu prepared her tea and got her to take aspirin and lie down.

I finished up packing. When I came to bed, Basha was staring out the window, at the torn clouds. Her face was the kind of thing one sees in the classical wing of a museum: beauty as a force of history. Her robe rode up the back of her thighs. I had it in mind that we might make love. That was what my great, quivering cliché of a body had in mind.

I climbed onto the bed and curled around her from behind and nuzzled against her bottom. "It's our last night together," I said.

Basha shook her head.

"Honey," I whispered. "Please."

"Don't," she said softly. "No."

"I just want to love you." I pressed myself against her.

This was the wrong move. I knew that. But I felt, at that moment, as if I had nothing else to fall back on. Our affair—our grand drama of abandonment and reclamation—had run aground. It was time for our bodies to leap to the rescue.

Basha, for all her evasions, was ahead of me there. She understood that the body can only express wishes. It cannot undo facts. "No," she said. "Leave me alone."

What sort of comment was this? *Leave me alone?* We were lovers. This was our last night. I stared at Basha's long, slender legs. Her skin seemed to grow more and more pale, as if she were dissolving into the sheets. But I didn't want her to go yet. My hand reached for the stem of her neck.

Basha began to weep. "Stop," she said. "Don't touch me."

"Does that hurt?" I pressed at the warm cords of muscle. "Am I hurting you?"

Suddenly Basha was kicking at me, the robe riding up until I could see the cleft of her ass, her lovely white halves tensing, the fine hairs and skin darkening to blue in the furrow. I knew what I wanted to do. It was perfectly clear. I grabbed her hips.

Basha's elbow swung back, knocked me in the mouth, and I could taste blood now, a good taste, sweet and full of ruin. Basha wriggled away and got up from the bed. I might have leapt up, pursued her, done God knows what. But I could see, through the frosted glass of the door, Mamu hovering just outside.

"Run away," I said. "That's right, run away."

"You're the one," Basha sobbed. She opened the door and collapsed into her mother and the two of them stood there for a minute. Then they moved off, like a pair of wounded soldiers, and I heard the door to Mamu's room swing shut.

I waited for my breathing to subside, then went and stood outside the door. I could hear the two of them, whispering in Polish. I opened the door, but neither of them bothered to turn. Mamu reached to straighten the compress she had laid along her daughter's brow. Basha whimpered, in the manner of a child struggling toward sleep. She held the hem of Mamu's skirt in her fist. And I understood, now, why Mamu had never resented my presence: she knew Basha would never forsake her, not in the end.

Mamu emerged from Basha's room an hour later. I was in the kitchen, staring at the empty courtyard below. She smiled politely and took a Petit Ceour from the pack stashed in the cupboard. "Maybe you like sandwich for the trip?"

"That's okay," I said.

But already she was reaching into the fridge, removing a hunk of cheese, some kielbasa wrapped in foil, pulling a knife from the magnetized strip above my head. The skin of her hands was like beautiful pink paper.

"She's asleep?"

Mamu nodded.

"Maybe I should sleep on the couch?"

Mamu shrugged. She sliced the kielbasa and the cheese and layered them on the roll. "You have made all your suitcases?"

I nodded. I could feel the swell of my fat lip.

"I guess I might have hurt her," I said. "I was pretty angry. You know, having to leave and all. We're both a little crazy."

Mamu gazed at me. Smoke drifted from her nose. She had known this was coming, after all. Men were people who left; they were not dependable. Their other charms, their money and their words and their cocks, these were only temporary compensations. Her daughter was finally learning this.

Later, there would be another soggy good-bye, lurid with airport hope. And later still, the letters and phone calls, which slipped to hollow, fainter in their promise, until they vanished altogether. Basha was not the sort to cling, not the sort I might dial up in the small hours, with a bit too much wine and night in me, to make sure she was still somehow stuck. There is a point you reach, I mean, when you are just something bad that happened to someone else.

"I'm sorry," I said. "I'm sorry for everything."

But Mamu wasn't angry. It would be no easier for me in the end. And so she came to me, stepped around the table and gathered me into her arms, and I buried my head in her bosom, which smelled of smoke and laundry soap and ten thousand meals, and began to sob, for Basha, for Mamu, for all of us in the suffering of our desires.

The Law of Sugar

The thing I had to realize was that all the laws kept changing. That was why Matesh was recommending Polish sugar. "Very unstable law," he said, as if I had disagreed. "With all the elections. Ha! Politicians are shit. So why are you going to risk? If you cannot protect?"

"A good point," I said again. "But now, I think, I must go."

"With sugar there is an *agreement*," Matesh said, pounding his fist on the table. "There is the guarantee." He called out for more drinks, but the waiter ignored him. I reminded him that it was getting late, I had to go.

"Prague? Fuck Prague. Too much Germans already. Hungary? Too much mafias. Poland. This is the place! But not for buildings. Foreigners are not allowed to own the lands here. And with the elections, all the laws will change. So? So?" He looked at me with devout expectancy, like a child awaiting dessert.

"Sugar?"

"Yes! Sugar! Sugar!" He clinched with laughter. It seemed so obvious, so desirable.

The waiter made his way over with three more beers. Matesh clapped his tiny hands. "Good beer. *Polish* beer." He muttered something to the waiter, who wiped his hands on his apron grumpily. I pulled another bill from my wallet, but Matesh shook his head. He picked coins from his pocket, one after another, and handed them to the waiter.

"Please," I said. "Let me."

"It is too late." Matesh waved the waiter off.

"Yes," I said. "That's quite true."

Matesh's sister sipped her beer. She was lovely, as pale and smooth as new cobblestone.

Out beyond the cafe railing, girls strolled the square in short dresses and young men stumbled after them. Dusk was arriving and still everyone wore sunglasses. A man, apparently blind, played an eerie tune on his recorder. Dogs of indeterminate breed began swirling at the far edge of the plaza.

"You establish a fund for all this," Matesh said. "To protect your monies."

"I haven't got any monies," I said. "I'm a librarian."

Matesh nodded. He was delighted at my disavowals, taking them as an indication of vast wealth and acumen. "Then there is one person who manages your fund, and you are sent dividends. Dividends, yes? The monies from your risk."

"Yes," I said. "That sounds quite good. I would like to think about it."

"What is thinking?" Matesh said. "Thinking is shit. While you think, the Germans move in. They are awful. I have met them. They will make all the money in sugar. Our money." Matesh fished for a cigarette, which seemed lit even as he drew it from the pack. He inhaled regally.

Matesh's sister smiled. She had crooked teeth and splendid pink gums. I detected the hint of an apology in her expression. I gazed at my beer.

"People will always need sugar," Matesh announced. "For cakes and candies and ice creams. The parliament knows this, so they have made an agreement." He tapped his head. "This law never changes, the law of sugar. If they change this, then what? No sugar! No cakes! Nothing!"

"Yes," I said, having a swallow of beer. "I see."

"What is a world without sugar?"

I checked my watch and felt a great gladness I had left my bag back at the hotel.

"People need sugar. This will not go away. Even if the communists are elected again. The communists need sugar also!"

"Everyone needs sugar," I said. "Let me think about it."

"What is to think?" Matesh said sharply.

I felt something brush against my leg and noticed Matesh's sister release into the air a delicate sigh.

A group of street performers had congregated at the center of the square, and one of them, obviously quite drunk, was spitting fire using a bottle of clear alcohol with an old wick. It was the fire that attracted the dogs, I think. That, or the blind man's piping. I watched them establish flanks and begin a run.

"This doesn't take long," Matesh said. "A few months, no more. And then we are rich. Or, if you like, a year. Even richer. I have helped many men. There are others who would make you wait for many years. I do not. How it begins is what you call a wire transfer. 'Wire transfer,' yes? No one sees the wire. They are just numbers in a bank. Ha!"

"I'm a librarian," I said. "I work in a library."

"Yes," Matesh said. "Like in the library. But not taking books. Taking sugar!"

The dogs were making noise now. Not barks, or snarls, but a kind of a throttled hum. "In the last year, the beets were excellent.

But this year, not enough beets. Not much beets, not much sugar! You see? The prices go up up up."

Matesh's sister had caught sight of the dogs. She had sunglasses on, but you could see she wasn't happy about it. She whispered to Matesh, but he waved his cigarette, erasing her with smoke. The waiter stationed at the entrance of the cafe adopted a look of slight concern and began stacking the thick wooden chairs. He shouted at the blind man to stop playing. The blind man nodded in acknowledgment, and began playing louder.

The dogs had reached the street performers. One clamped on to the leg of the master of ceremonies and the tumblers circled them, leaping and yipping pointlessly. The couples who had gathered around began edging backward. Only the intervention of the man breathing fire brought the attack to an end.

"Once you are in with the sugar," Matesh said, leaning toward me, "this can lead to other risks. *Good* risks."

"The dogs," I said. "They seem to be heading this direction."

"It is not worth waiting," Matesh assured me. "Some risks are too good. If you wait, they are gone. With the wheat, during the time of Jimmy Carter, it was like this. You wait and it is over. Gone. *Poof.*"

The dogs were moving now with real assurance, carving a path across the plaza. I didn't know what to do. I didn't even know how I had wound up here. I wanted to tell someone there had been a mistake. Rather a large one. But in these situations who does one tell? The waiter stepped inside and bolted the door, locking us out. The young men and women of the plaza dispersed. The blind fellow continued to play, but falteringly, dipping his chin, as if someone were yanking at his beard. I began casting about for a nearby corner.

"This is where connections become necessary," Matesh said. He was back to tapping his head. "Not for the law, because this does not change. But to make sure that we have the position we need. There are, perhaps, others who would like our position."

The dogs had set upon someone, or something. You could see their muzzles knifing in, tattering a bright fabric. They sounded serious and awfully happy. I strained for a better look, but Matesh kept his head in front of mine. His nose was the color of wet brick.

"Really," I said. "I think it best if we go."

"There is no need for a contract," Matesh decided. "Perhaps if you were German, but we are gentlemen here."

"The dogs," I said.

"A contract is shit," Matesh said.

I stood and held out my hand. "So, really——." Matesh finished his beer, frowning.

The dogs were through with whatever it had been and were now scouring the cafe two down from ours. I could see their fangs and a bit of froth. I stood for a moment longer, offering my hand, but Matesh seemed downcast. An air of tragedy descended onto him. His suit, which had looked so shiny an hour ago, now appeared dull and uninhabited. One of the smaller dogs, a kind of terrier, leaped onto the railing a few tables away. My hand hung in the air. And hung. It felt dead, felt connected to other dead parts.

And then, as these things sometimes happen, it did: Matesh's sister reached out and took my hand and rose to her feet, like a long stem. Quite quickly, we were gone. It was the first time I had run in weeks, months, and her hand, in mine, felt new and alive. Behind us we could hear Matesh. He was scolding the dogs. "What are you?" he shouted. "You are dogs. You know nothing of risks."

Matesh's sister was fleet and she knew the streets and I feel confident in saying there is no man on this green, green earth who could have kept me from following her, just then.

The Pass

A man in a bar makes a pass at a woman. It's not a good era for passes, but he's giving it his all. His eyebrows have been laying groundwork for hours. His voice—a nice voice he's been told, a *radio* voice—lingers on her name. She's on her third drink and she's here, isn't she, with him, and not somewhere else and she's finally removed the purse from her lap, on which it had sat like a small guard dog.

They're downtown someplace, some downtown, some place, the skyscrapers blazing like exorbitant lamps, subway trains hurling their human cargo past, lakewind breathing concrete and car exhaust, dusk punching out.

He's Bill or Mike or Chuck. She's Rachel, Liz, Michele with one *l*. She has a beautiful name. He's told her so and now leans in, close enough to smell the Clamato on her breath. He hopes to appear smooth and audacious. Like Brando, or Valentino. She stirs her Bloody Mary with an odd precision, as if being evaluated.

He touches her arm with just his fingertips. Will she consent to the pleasure they might take in all this: the lifting of their bodies, the lying of them down, the pale revelations, wetness dispatched outward, all of it? With his hand and mouth, both, he asks her to share in the complicated electricity of the moment.

They have met before, these two—or two very much like them—at a costume party several years ago. She was dressed as Salome, with seven veils and a wispy black bra. He was a caveman. She lowered her painted eyes and spoke in the way of a biblical moll. He said *unga-bunga-bunga*. She swung her hips and made her veils flutter. He dragged her by the hair to a dark back room; wishes he had.

But why a bad era for the pass?

Because the pass is what semioticians would call a *lapsed signifier*. That which once defined the act—an attempted breach of the culture's sexual mores—has been overrun by the horny course of human affairs. It is not that nothing is sacred anymore. On the contrary. More is sacred than ever before, because more of the self is hidden away than ever before. But the pass no longer aims in the direction of anything hidden. It has become overt, incurably so.

A woman awaits her flight to Denver; efficiently rouged, screwed into a stylish black pantsuit. But thunderheads have kicked up and those ninnies at the FAA have the incomings circling and God knows how long this will take, so she repairs to the eager banter of the terminal bar. She is a woman slightly older than her initial impression, shrewd in the matter of lighting. She settles in at the dim end of the teakwood bar, next to a man in a rumpled suit, another captive, and orders a screwdriver.

They are not drinkers, but they have time on their hands, and now the communion of ill tempers. Judgment is passed on the vagaries of their airline, the bartender's chest hair, the focus-group decor. Intolerances line up nicely. Together, they listen to a New York matron bellow into a pay phone, sounding like a motherless calf. He makes a gentle observation about the indolence of the janitorial staff.

On the wall above them: a poster of *Casablanca*, Bogie and Ingrid on that backlot tarmac, draped in pink fog, doing their utmost to dignify lurid hope. And outside, in the crowded bay beyond the X-ray machines: couples trapped in farewell holding patterns, wearing travel outfits and travel hairdos and lip gloss, the women smudgy, the men guarding good-bye erections.

He has a certain gangster handsomeness, Mr. Rumpled Suit, his broad face pressed back, a nose she imagines has been broken, clear brown eyes. His hands are large and pleasantly scarred. Around his ring finger, not a ring, but a pale band. She orders another screwdriver. He hurries off in search of information about departure times. (He has a deposition to oversee in Pittsburgh.)

She finds that she misses him. Odd. Yet there can be no other way to explain the elation she feels when she spots him edging past the luggage cart return rack, his rumpled trousers and, inside them, his thick legs.

"Bad news," he says. "I have a wife."

Or: "We will only hurt one another."

Or, just possibly: "No more outgoing flights." In this third case, her hand will slip onto his thigh for the joy of feeling astonished movement under her fingers, flesh awaiting further instruction.

But these are strangers and the possibilities of the pass tempt them with no afterthought.

At a party in a suburb renowned for its outdoor sculpture, a group of coworkers share red wine and veggie dip. They know one another in the way modern workers do, a forced animation of concern. Some are married and others single and each group covets the other. A life too full of choices has rendered them indecisive. They are prosperous on the scale of their parents, but lack the rootedness that might fortify their hopes. They live in apartments and spend hours on the phone, deciding things. Where to eat. What movie to see. They enter into relationships that feel, as much as anything, like arrangements. They are poorly versed in the mechanics of regret.

In this domain the pass acquires something of a darkling's charm. The man about to make the pass, Geoff, is seated at the center of a comfy living room. The woman, Elena, is on the couch above him. She has the face of a Modigliani, exotically crooked, long and pale, cow-eyed. There has been speculation about her breasts in the office—they sit suspiciously high—but he is more taken by her backside, which is plump, cupidinous.

Elena's boyfriend is in the kitchen. He is a nice fellow with a large mole on his chin. He sometimes makes the mistakes of his small-town rearing, a certain misguided exuberance in dressing or off-color joke. Geoff's girlfriend, on the stairs, is a sophisticate, versed in city tropes, an unembarrassed practitioner of seduction. When Geoff first started sleeping with her, her fierce scatology, the way she demanded to be slapped, thrilled him. More recently, he finds her vehemence frightening. They are a happy couple, Geoff supposes, as happy as couples tend to be.

But there is an innocence about Elena that pricks his vanity, makes him jumpy for what he doesn't have. She is tipsy and agreeable and words are his allies. He steers the conversation toward intimate topics: massages, body piercing, sensual ambition.

I think you know some things, he tells her. I watch you move through the office and I think you know some things that most people wouldn't think you know.

She rolls her eyes.

So many guys talk about your chest. I'm sorry. I don't mean to embarrass you. Please don't be embarrassed. There's a loveliness there that makes them curious. That's all. You can't blame them for that. But I think they're missing it, Elena. I think with you it's the lower body, the *nalgas.* I've been meaning to tell you this for a while. I know it's not right, but I watch you walk through the office, the way you move, and I think: I'm not sure I can go through my life without knowing.

And there are provinces in which everyone does go about finding out, clusters of college graduates knotted at the bottom of tall cities, trying to invent community. Everyone has slept with everyone and they all drink together, hoping the alcohol and the music will restore some previously eluded glamour, or obscure its dissipation. Those few who haven't coupled operate at a disadvantage, edgy and prideful, untrammeled by ease. They watch the others sweat and sway, and imagine a daisy chain of limbs, themselves missing out. In this stewing lies the seed of future passes.

But what lies ahead is not our concern. Our concern is the present, the glorious now, the moment of erotic transfer—isotopic, dangling, a question mark awaiting exclamation.

*   *   *

In a rundown Stuttgart nightclub, two privates in the U.S. Army have arrived to hear jazz, arrived separately. They are from different divisions, have never met. The club is in the historic district, miles from the biergartens where their comrades fill themselves with liters of pale pilsner and oily sausage, counting colored bills for later descent on the hookers of this drizzled ashen city.

Technically, it's not even jazz on display in this blue-lit club. It's cabaret, the music of campy self-announcement, feather boas and top hats and tulle stockings and whorish makeup, and each of the privates drinks in the burly innuendo, sipping at sophisticated drinks, sneaking glances at each other, wondering. Between acts, the one named Shane spots the other leaning against the bar, uniform neatly tucked, back curving gracefully, the muscles under his shirt shifting like dunes.

Shane bites a piece of ice, moves to join him. They talk about where they are stationed, what their hitch is—awkward, beginning things. The lights vanish and another round of drinks gets drunk and another set of skits begins, more good-time tunes set against a black velvet curtain, a tall tenor with pasted-on mustache and a chanteuse treated rather sadly by the years (though, they agree, surely lovely as a maiden).

The hours roll by and the drinks loosen them and soon they are confessing which high school shows they were in, bursting into stagy refrains. The hour is close to curfew, but the closing spectacle is more than either private could have expected. The old singer is up on the bar flashing her fallen thighs and the tenor is leaping from table to table in patent-leather wing tips and the two privates are suddenly at the center of a spotlight with a microphone under their chins, thrown together in voice, led laughing through a wobbly chorus of *Auf Widersahn* by the older patrons.

Shane turns to his new companion and breathes the hot breath of want and with nothing so much as this asks to be folded into this stranger's body and kept there for the night.

This is what the whole business is about: night. Without night, its hungering canvas, its needy musk and daring sediments, without all this, the amorous among us would fold our tents and, like Long-fellow's Arabs, as silently steal away.

He met her through a mutual friend and now she is in his home and he is cooking for her, chopping mushrooms and boiling water for pasta, washing the cupboard dust off his wineglasses. He has learned to cook a few meals from TV chefs and knit these into the tight circle of his life. His business—consulting—sucks him through airports and phones and flights and conferences and beepers and burgers and sour suits and occasionally he suspects he is missing something. Not daughters or wives or azaleas, but the sense of his body as experienced against another. Night illuminates this need, tenders it, demands a dividend.

This woman in his apartment, she is—what? A nurse or a stenographer. A piano teacher. She exhibits patience worthy of a bygone era. He sees her traveling the Oregon Trail in a long plain dress, mending things. Her fingers are strong, able-looking. There is something steadying just in the way she holds her chardonnay, cupped in both hands. She leans against the fridge carefully. Her eyes seem to want to dip beneath the surface of his words, toward more telling information.

She is not someone he thinks of as pretty. There are flaws, which his life surrounded by advertising draws out, distorts. Slight underbite. Flat bottom. Saggy arms. The defects are not small. But then, there is him. Sometimes, before bed, he catches sight of himself in the bathroom mirror and sees his father.

They are here because he invited her. Night fell around him, his first one home after a cross-country trip, and something in the yellowing of the streetlamps outside his building left him bereft. He remembered his friend pressing this woman's number onto him, how he had avoided calling her, thinking: *she must be desperate.* When he finally got her on the phone, two nights later, he was the one who felt desperate, trying to play the idea off as an impulse.

He continues to chop and she pours herself more wine and moves around his apartment, inspecting. He knows about her: she has been married before, she has a child who is away for the week, she is the same age he is. He knows *about* her. She glances at his stack of unopened mail, as if she would like to sort through it, as if she doesn't quite trust him to separate the junk from the significant.

He puts the knife down and tilts up his wine, stopping when he feels a slight burn against his gums. He slips out of his shoes and approaches her from behind and her neck is there, warm. He knows this could happen only from behind, that he is sneaking up on himself as much as her. He closes his eyes and hopes.

Or a wedding. Sure. Why not? They still hold them. Big distracted churchy affairs glittering with pearls or earnest runty ones on damp lawns. The nudnik photographer, the sweaty caterers, weeping mothers and black sheep beckoned back, the bow-tied band and the bride and groom helpless with goodwill. It still goes on in all these places, San Leandro and Mount Kisco and Wallingford, and, at the fringe of it, behind the rectory or out near the pool, a bridesmaid stares ardently at a groomsman. They have had much to drink, as weddings recommend.

She is so proud of her friend, she says, and the groomsman agrees. It is something to be proud of. She is so beautiful. Yes. Never seen her so radiant. Yes. Beautiful. And him, too. He didn't look so tall in the photos. How tall is he? Six-foot-three. Wow.

He is thinking about the bachelor party, about the stripper called Danielle, between whose breasts his nose spent a brief and thrilling span, shocked at the scent (shoe leather and cinnamon) and the firmness of whatever held them aloft. This moony bridesmaid—with her wedge of a face and colored contacts, her peach chiffon dress and matching pumps—she is no Danielle. She is a creature in sad real time. Her nakedness cannot be anything men would pay to see, though men, if protected by payment, will look at almost anything.

And anyway, she is here before him, full of crab ravioli and champagne, swallowing back burps and twisting her bangs between her fingers. She hasn't the will to execute the pass. She can only display her markings, touch her body in ways that might induce in him a mimetic response.

He is at his leisure to consider this, to ease back on his ankles and assess the pros and cons. She is homely; there is that. Yet her homeliness weighs on him favorably, accents his moderate beauty. This is a wedding and there is drink and hopes run deep on such occasions, but not so expectations. All pageantry inspires fantasy, no matter how shabby. And besides, she is wearing these prim peach pumps, shoes that will never be used again, which almost demand to be torn off, bitten at in mock depravity.

He is not certain about kissing, though, not just yet. And so he lowers his hand down the front of her dress and lifts her breast so that it puddles on his palm and so that he can hear his name on her tongue.

In every life, such deciding places must be reached. Especially in this era of frantic indecision, with its impatient sun and hammering moon, with its pathological ulteriority, when it seems a wonder that two people might ever agree to anything like terms. Day after fallen day, these odd delicious moments on which so much depends; unwrapped like papered pears, held close to nose, sniffed, tasted.

In the downtown bar, where Bill or Mike or Chuck has pinned his hopes on the sleeve of Rachel, Liz, Michele: a failure he could not have foreseen. (For if he had, why should he have invited her here and spent his money and time and dwindling predator energy?) She looks at his hand on her arm and smiles politely. She sighs, and in her sigh invokes the nearest cliché: nothing personal a bad time still recovering just met someone.

He envisions her dressed as Salome, the dance of her veils. If this were physical trauma, the endorphins would come sloshing in to spare him. He would not hear the chant of looming humiliation, or feel suffused by brittle hate for this woman, who is no longer a woman, only something he will never have. The electricity in his arm, with which he hoped to jolt her into panting collaboration, shuts down. The bartender freezes. The skyscrapers go dark. The set is struck.

* * *

The airport pair have no such trouble. The airlines, after all, have arranged passage to a nearby hotel. Inside his room, the man who looks like a gangster shucks his suit, steps into the shower, pleased at the water's scalding pulse, emerging pink, soapy. On his bed: the woman who missed her flight to Denver. She is in towels, one around her chest, one twirled on her head. Older with her makeup scrubbed, her flesh unbundled. Nothing like Ingrid Bergman, with her slender white nose and her shadows. Nothing like his wife for that matter, who drinks protein shakes and runs half-marathons. Nothing like anyone he could have ever seen himself lying beside in a hotel room near the airport. And for this reason, an object of intense fascination to his body, which responds along predictable lines. They are not graceful, or pretty. He lunges, she groans. They press together. The entire project fills no more than a few minutes. But when he reaches for one of her cast-away towels she grabs his wrist. "Wait," she says. "I like to let it dry."

This, more than anything, more than his refusal to bestow upon her a goodnight kiss, more than his stiff retreat from her mouth, more than the silent next-morning shuttle ride, will haunt him. He has always worried that he looks like a thug, ever since his nose was broken by a bully in high school. The sight of his ejaculate spattered on her belly jolts loose a memory, this bully staring hard at a pornographic photo in a mildewy gym, now thirty years ago, announcing: *That broad is a waste of good sperm.*

And what of Geoff, at the center of the warm suburban home unspooling his patter to Elena, who looks like a Modigliani? He too has misjudged. And he too will suffer a mortification, though not of the flesh. He reaches for her ankle and she pulls away and his chest stumbles. She stands quickly and moves to join her boyfriend in the kitchen. Soon it will be announced to those assembled that the couple are engaged. And still later he will see the two of them outside, nuzzling against a car.

Closer to morning, with his own girlfriend curled away from him, Geoff will see things as they are: that he coveted Elena's innocence not as a thing to defile but as a remedy. Beneath the fantasy of ravaging her was the fantasy that she would rescue him, stroke his brow and somehow cure him of his tired contempt for everything. With her, he might have become the sort of man who desires purely, rather than the sort who seeks betrayal at the center of a foolish party. He will never feel quite sure of himself again.

The old torch singer is surprised and pleased by the presence of two young American soldiers. She dispatches the proprietor of the club to invite them backstage: the madame would like to say hello after she has changed. PFC Shane and his companion are led to a small room with a single old love seat. The light is soft, roseate. There is the pleasant, cherryish smell of pipe tobacco. Their thighs brush.

But now Shane wonders if this might not be an elaborate setup. He has heard tell of such things, MPs descending with billy clubs. Then, too, there is the ambiguity of his new friend's responses: a fluttery hug in the shadows, that lopsided grin, which could mean anything. When you are a soldier like PFC Shane, you learn to love quickly, to grasp and gulp and be done with it. Besides, there is the curfew to be considered.

Now the diva makes her appearance, shorter than she seemed on the bar, modestly wrapped in a chenille robe. French cigarettes in a silver case. A cocktail in a tall goblet. She lived for a number of years in Houston, Texas. Do they know the place? An oil baron kept her as his mistress. All quite scandalous. She was terribly lonely in her glass and marble flat on Carr Street, like a princess in her tower. This *awl* baron—her imitation makes them giggle—used to come and pounce on her. Fat and hairy as a woodchuck, with a prick like a jackass. When you are young, she says, it all seems enough. But love is the most important thing of all, don't you agree? How old are you boys? Really, that young? Well it's time you learned the first rule of love: Never hide. Love must be acknowledged by the touch of days. And here she makes her exit, leaving them her dressing room and the time to decide for themselves.

What a trip, Shane says.

Yeah, says his new friend. Pretty amazing. The boy's arm falls across Shane's shoulders. His mouth is a wet red arrow.

Yeah.

The consultant has placed his lips to her neck and she has responded with the consent of her body, turning against him, lifting her face. She is there and ready. But now he is unsure. The pass sits wrong with him, plunging dread where the flutter should be. All he can imagine is the moment after physical release, when the soul, the patient soul, reasserts sovereignty. This is the war that never ends: the body's simple needs set against the soul's byzantine wants, each accusing the other of insufficient grace.

No. No pass should suffer such sad scrutiny. She senses the slackening of his muscles and slumps onto the couch. It is called a pass because there is a movement of one desire past another. But the desires of this couple sit still as stone and stare down on both of them and the best they can manage is a kind of dour truce.

We should do this again, the consultant says.

Sure, the piano teacher says. I'd like that.

There is a long pause. He doesn't know what to do with this. In his off-site seminars they tell him to attack the lulls, tell a joke, make a comment about the weather. But listening to the sad uncertain timbre of her voice ruins his focus.

Anyway, he says.

Right, she says. Sure.

The young couple at the wedding, the bridesmaid and the groomsman, they have no such difficulties. Not yet. For the moment, they are tongues and tails and hips and hands. The arm of night lowers itself over the rectory, turns the swimming pool into a small blue jewel. They have pressed themselves against the side of a building, tumbled into the shallow end, staggered to the nearest flat surface; her peach chiffon dress is bunched around her thighs, his rented gray suit has split down the middle.

The body, the body, the body. And the dizzy players that spin across this smooth field. They are all of them to be applauded. Nights *are* long. An entire lifetime of long. And the pass, here, now, a merciful lantern which lights the way, softly dims, and drags us toward dream.

MOSCOW

She told him: "I am completely naked."

These were the first words she spoke and they tumbled from her mouth, beautifully shaped, smoothed by an accent which sounded French, but was from farther east, Moscow, so that what he heard was: *Ah im compledly neggid.* Her voice rose slightly, placed emphasis on the third word, as if her nakedness were a gift meant entirely for him, presented without forethought, without the least awareness of the rougher ends to which such declarations can be put.

They were on a thin, hissing phone line. She might have been speaking from fifty years ago. He closed his eyes. And as he did, she slipped into a new kind of nakedness, a nakedness untainted by the body's awful math, restored to classical grace. He saw white breasts, plucked from the white of her chest, her high bottom, the soft furrows of her rib cage. He saw her on tiptoe. He saw her lips make the words in wide, red bands.

He understood that what she said was not intended as titillation, even coy provocation. It was merely a happy coincidence. The phone rang and, in her urgent hope that it be him, she picked the receiver up, forgetting to cover herself, forgetting that she stood, in her apartment, in Moscow, without a stitch of clothing. It was an act of forgetting, then. And her statement to him, an act of delighted remembrance.

He desired in her this wondrous capacity, no hint of which she had shown him previously, that she would someday grow so accustomed to him, so unembarrassed by her own physicality, that she would forget, and then remember, her own nakedness, that just such a cycle might mark their days together. Hearing her words, he felt transported above shame, above lust and privation. If the moment could be clung to, sustained like a perfect note. Perhaps Moscow was such a place. Perhaps there, such possibilities existed.

He had never visited, had only seen photos: grim, towering statues, wide streets, open squares, and, on the horizon, church spires of the oddest shape, like clumps of wet chocolate drawn to a point. Perhaps Moscow was banked in snow, and perhaps the heat of her pale body, standing beside a window, caused the pane to fog.

But even as this image formed, a second image took shape, of him below her window, outside, staring up. And here, from this vantage point, she grew blurry, obscured not by some trick of condensation, or light or distance, but his own insistent longing.

Hardly any time had passed since she spoke, but now he could not see her at all, not as she had existed before. He felt the hard knock of need, stiffened against himself. He might have reached out, tried to explain to her what was happening, but he didn't understand himself. A singular vision of love was perfecting itself in the singular shape of her. And yet that shape, by its very recognition, was now receding, dissolving, and reemerging as something else, a myth of his own illusive want, a creature with a thatch of glistening pubic hair, a crude mouth, nipples the color of bruises.

Years later he toured the factory in Hershey, Pennsylvania. It was late and he was the only visitor, and the guide—a young woman in a severe suit—walked him briskly through each cavernous room. Workers in surgical scrubs scurried to and fro. Steel machines hissed and banged and choked. He watched one dip down and release through invisible apertures a thousand coins of chocolate, then pull away so violently as to bring these to a sharp, liquid point. The process was repeated time and again, a mass production of the inimitable, which seemed to him, in that moment, terribly wrong.

He hadn't loved her in the beginning. He was sure of that. He may never have loved her for more than that one, long-ago moment.

But now, as he watched the spires of Moscow reproduced in miniature, as the guide hustled him along toward a bin with free chocolates, urging him to select one-just-one-now-is-the-moment-sir-*please*, coldly appraising his dazed expression; now, as he staggered toward the bin and obediently removed a piece, as he exited into the frigid parking lot, as he tore at the foil, as the chocolate fell into his mouth through a puff of steamy breath and began at once to seep away; now he recognized that he would never rid himself of the moment. It was insoluble.

He had suffered, without a doubt, one perfect memory which, though misplaced, had never been forgotten. It lived inside him and would continue to do so for the rest of his life, to be reawakened again and again. And so he got into his car and drove on the turnpike and exited and turned into a field and stopped the car and stepped outside and removed each piece of his clothing and lay down in the banked snow and waited for Moscow—the cold lips of that distant city—to brush his skin.

Valentino

We were at this party, was the situation. Holden was holding forth on his theory of beauty gradients. "You can't get out of your depth aesthetically," he said. "You do that and you're done for."

"I've heard this before," I said. "I know all this."

"All men and women are divided along aesthetic lines, see. That's just the way it is. There's maybe twenty, twenty-two such strata. At the top you've got the movie stars and models, okay? Tom Cruise and that skinny bitch he's married to, all those fuckers. Then the soap stars and TV anchors. Then commercial actors, then actual nontelevised attractive people, down to the average, sort of ugly, and at the bottom the real sad cases, cleft palates and the like."

"Right." I watched Astrid Miller make her way toward the keg.

"The trick here is that every person recognizes intuitively where they belong on the beauty gradient. This is the first thing you gauge when you walk into a room. Right? It's like: 'Okay, better than him, worse than him, way better than him.' That's how people know who they're supposed to end up with. It's like that song about Noah: *The animals, they came on, they came on in twosies, twosies.*"

"Wait a sec," I said. "That's about species. Species of animals."

Holden tapped his temple. "That's what they *tell* you it's about, man. That song's about who gets fucked by who. That's what that whole thing is *about*."

"You're so full of shit," I said.

"If I'm so full of shit, how do you explain Kim Forrest and DeWitt Henderson?" This was Holden's trump card, and he displayed it with a princely fluttering of his hands.

Kim Forrest was the hottest girl at our high school. She had run through most of the varsity captains by sophomore year, but never gone all the way. Then this guy, DeWitt Henderson, transferred to our school. He was droopy-eyed and blond, full of hunky grace. All year they circled each other. And the way we heard the story—a story so often repeated it had become, among our pathetic stratum, a kind of masturbatory liturgy—when they finally hooked up, out behind the old grange silo, Kim came not once, not twice, but four times, and was so dazzled by DeWitt's sexual sangfroid that, lying in his arms afterward, she wept with gratitude.

"You think that happens to anyone other than Henderson?" Holden said. "No way. Kim Forrest was saving herself for the guy who was her match on the beauty gradient. But the whole time she's waiting, see, she's getting more and more lathered up. She's like a bottle of Don Perignon that's been shaken for months, right? So when she finally gets popped—*kaboom*."

"What about different cultures?" I said. "You gonna tell me the bushmen of the Kalahari lust after Kim Forrest?"

"I didn't say that. You'd probably like it if I did, because you'd probably like a shot at some of that dusty Kalahari pussy. But I'm not saying that. The beauty gradient is a cultural determinant, my friend. But there ain't a culture that's exempt. The whole world, right down to fucking Nashua Point, Iowa, runs on a beauty gradient."

I knew this well enough. My mother, after all, had once been the most beautiful woman in Nashua. This beauty was what spared her when her mind began to unravel five years ago. She had always been an eccentric, strolling the aisles of the grocery store in her bathrobe, humming tunes in public. It was when she began lighting small fires in the front yard and picketing the phone company that my father sought professional help. He was sickened by her blooming madness. And yet the rest of Nashua treated her gently, like a princess who wanders from her throne and lies down to sleep amid the cows. My own grandparents, who had settled Nashua when it was just corn and fences, refused to acknowledge their daughter's condition. They were astounded when my father left.

"I'm trying to teach you something here," Holden said. "Just look at the instant case. Look at your pal Astrid." Astrid was the first girl I had ever kissed, on the spidery blacktop of Palmer elementary. "Astrid's getting herself in trouble right now," Holden said. "Even as we speak."

"How's that?"

"She's making a play for Scott Milikan, right?"

"Who says?"

"Everyone knows this. Shit, look at the rack." Astrid was wearing a red, velvety-type shirt about three sizes too small.

"So?"

"So she's in trouble. Milikan's out of her range. He's at least three, four grades up on the gradient."

This was true. Astrid, with her chunky frame and underbite, was no match for Milikan. He had a boxy jaw full of boxy teeth and tussled blond hair. Plus, he played soccer. He started ahead of me at sweeper.

"Who says Ast can't get him? She looks good tonight."

"I'm not saying she can't get him. That's not what I'm saying. What I'm saying is, she won't be able to keep him."

Astrid sipped her beer and laughed. Milikan was a few steps away, pumping the keg, smiling, a man with options.

"Everyone knows Ast is making a play for him, and he knows it too. Don't you doubt it. He's got a few beers in him and he's sizing her up, mostly around the hogans. Sure, Milikan's saying, why the hell not? Problem is, he's not in it for the long haul. Beer can blur the picture, but it can't repaint the lines."

"What about personality?" I said. "Personality counts for something."

"Not compared to looks. The only thing that beats looks is power or money. For crying out loud, Tommy, who do you think is getting laid in this country? Are you, my friend, in the great scheme of things, getting laid? No, you're getting various hues on *le palette de blue balls*. You know who's getting laid? Rock musicians. Politicians. Athletes. Why? Why are these men getting laid? Why are these often very ugly men getting laid? Because they've got at least two of the magic three. Dennis Rodman? You think anyone wants to fuck him if he's not Dennis Rodman? Bono? Bono is dog meat. Who fucked Bono before he was Bono? No one, that's who. Ugly chicks, maybe."

Astrid had left the keg. She was off somewhere, powdering something. Milikan was talking to another girl.

"And I must tell you, my friend, this is good sex we're talking about. Don't delude yourself into thinking the prime studage of this country is having substandard sex. No siree. They are having porn-quality, multi-gasm sex. They have fucked so many women, and women are so delighted to be fucking them, so moist at the idea of being part of the imprimatur, that these guys are getting hummers.

These women, when they suck these guys off, they're humming. Like the seven dwarfs. Humming while they work."

"The dwarfs whistled."

Holden and I had been best friends forever, though that was going to change soon because I was going East for college, while Holden—who was probably twice as smart as I was—was taking summer-school classes. He hoped to get his diploma in time to maybe enroll at Foothill, the local community college.

Milikan finally surrendered the keg, and I went to get more beer.

I felt a hip nudge me.

"Hey," I said.

Astrid showed me her lovely underbite. "Hey yourself."

"You look great."

"Oh Tommy. How sweet!" She gave me an exuberant little hug. You could tell she was sloshed. "How's the philosopher?"

"Oh, you know. As full of shit as ever."

Astrid smiled and I could see a lipstick stain on one of her front teeth. She glanced over my shoulder. Milikan was behind me, talking with this little blond, a sophomore. Astrid hugged me again and stumbled off toward Milikan.

"That looked enjoyable." Holden sniffed at me. "Did she spray you?"

"Drink your beer."

We stood there and watched Astrid and Milikan and the blond. Astrid was doing most of the talking, her boobs right out there, swaying like loose signage.

"She looks hot," I said.

"Not hot enough," Holden said. "Milikan ends up taking blondie home."

"Fuck you," I said.

*　*　*

Astrid left the party with Milikan, in his fucking Jeep Cherokee, wobbled out the door, doughy but triumphant.

"You were wrong," I said, as I climbed into Holden's car.

Holden shook his head and grinned in a way meant to indicate I had missed the point. "A war of attrition. That's all. Ast just set it right out there, said: *Here's what you get, bub. No games. No hassles. A one-night deal.* Blondie's biding her time. Smart girl."

"Shut up."

"The situation will correct itself," Holden said.

"What if Milikan likes Ast, huh? What if he falls for her? You ever consider that?"

"Won't happen."

"Why not?"

"Different strata, sonny boy."

"That's sick," I said. "You're one sick fucking bastard."

"What are you getting so worked up about?"

"I'm not worked up."

Holden rolled through a stop sign. "It's not like I invented the rules, all right? The beauty gradient's just something that's out there. Like photosynthesis. Wouldn't exist at all, if it was up to me. Shit. If it was up to me, girls would dig us doggy guys with personality, okay? But it's not up to me."

"Just drive."

I was drunk on about three beers and I hadn't liked watching the little drama unfold, blondie fluttering around Milikan in all her unattainable beauty and Astrid crowding him, her tits brushing his arm every few seconds. Girls never behaved that way around me.

"Look," Holden said, "if it's any consolation, I think Astrid is within your range."

"What's that supposed to mean?"

"It means what it means. You're a couple of notches down, but she's within your range. She likes that you're heading East to school. She thinks it shows character, you're not just sticking around here and going to State. She told me."

This pleased me. I myself was dreading school. As much as I hated Nashua, the idea of adjusting to a new city terrified me. Then I remembered Milikan, the muscles showing beneath his soccer sweats, his phony-ass teeth.

"Lot of good it did me tonight."

"Wait it out," Holden said. "We're in July. It's a long way till August."

"September. I leave September second."

"Right."

We were drifting down Alma, through flashing reds. Out beyond the strip malls was the corn, all that fucking corn, growing yellower by the day. I thought about my mom, wondered what kind of state she'd be in when I got home.

"What about you," I said. "Jenno looked good tonight, no?" Holden had been feebly circling Jenno Wilkes for months.

"Nah. I'm laying low for a while."

"What's that supposed to mean?"

Holden began tapping the steering wheel and shifted in his seat. "It means what it means, Kimosabe. Hey, did I ever tell you about Valentino?"

"Who?"

"Rudolph Valentino. The silent-film star."

I shrugged.

"You've seen pictures of him, right?"

"I don't think so."

"Sure you have."

Holden had this habit of never quite allowing me to not know something.

"So tell me. Tell me about Randolph-fuckin-Valentino."

"Rudolph," Holden said. He was impossible to annoy. "All right, here's a guy who couldn't pay to get laid for most of his life. He was an Italian, right? Dark, swarthy type, like you. He grows up in this little town, down there in Sicily. And when he's about fifteen or something, his mom puts him on a ship to America. He can't speak a word of English, right? And he's living in this era that has zero tolerance for immigrants. So he gets to America and he's bumbling along, working as a ditchdigger out in L.A. A ditchdigger, for Chrissakes. Him and his Italian buddies. Just swinging a shovel, sweating all day in the sun and eating onion sandwiches."

"Onion sandwiches?" I said.

"He can't afford *meat*," Holden said. "Meat cost a lot of money back then. Anyway, one day this big-shot director spots him. They're doing a job out near the director's house. Digging a ditch. Valentino's humping along. His shirt's all sweat-stained and he hasn't shaved in like a month and he's puffing on a little Turkish cigarette. But this director, he sees something, some kind of special mark. He has his driver pull the car over and he calls out to Valentino, 'Young man. Young man!' All the other guys, the other Italians, they're whistling and hooting. Like: Who is this old fag? But three days later, Valentino is cast as the lead in his first movie. He goes on to become the single greatest sex symbol of the entire century. The gold standard of the male beauty gradient."

"Your point being?"

"Wait it out, Kimosabe. Tomorrow never knows."

"Very moving," I said. "Thanks." It was a strange story for Holden to tell, full of that ugly-duckling hopefulness that my mother was always pushing.

"Hey, lemme ask you a favor," Holden said quietly. "Can I crash at your place?"

"Sure."

Holden had problems with his stepdad. My mom didn't mind. She liked Holden. She said he had character.

I was working six days a week that summer, scooping ice cream at the Hungry Penguin. Holden was working construction with his stepdad, and this was not a pleasant situation. He didn't like for Holden to say anything, which was like telling a puppy not to wag its tail. Holden would never admit this, but the old man kind of bullied him around.

We went to all the lame parties that summer, the ones at Robbie Grove's and Carrie Madsen's and Trent Carmichael's and even one up in Porter Hills—which aren't really hills, just a plateau where the rich kids live. Holden used to live up there. His real dad had been a doctor.

The parties were always the same thing—a keg in the backyard, lots of milling around, maybe a few drunk girls dancing. This is just what we did. It gave our lives a focal point, however dim, and kept us locked within the social cloister of high school, where we felt safe to rail against the lives we were about to leave behind. Also, these parties were advertised as the only way to get laid in our town, however remote this possibility might have been in the case of Holden and myself.

My mother said nothing about my impending departure, though her behavior became increasingly erratic. Often I would return home to find her peeling the wallpaper with a steak knife, or painting designs on her arms with my old watercolor set. Her gaze was jittery and the meals she prepared were elaborate and nonsensical: mashed potatoes with chocolate fondue, Jell-O parmigiano.

She and Holden got along famously. I could hear them giggling over Scrabble, or assailing the late-night movie on Channel 39. They both talked back to the TV. If I returned from a party alone, my mother would inevitably look up and, with a certain lazy grimace caused by her medication, say: "Where's Holden?"

July's last party was thrown by my neighbor, Liz Wheaton. I was working late that night and had to race home on my bike to catch the end. I turned onto my street and saw someone walking, a girl in a short skirt and thick-soled sandals. I recognized those legs, which were thick and pale. It wasn't going to look good, me riding my old ten-speed, wearing a shirt with a little penguin holding a platter of ice cream. But I was thrilled at the chance to talk with Astrid alone.

I circled around and called out to her.

"Who is it?" She jerked a hand to her throat.

"It's me."

"God! Tommy, you scared me."

"Sorry. I'm sorry. I was just coming to see you."

"Well, here I am." I couldn't quite make out her face, which was hidden in the shadows cast by the mulberry trees.

"How was the party?"

"The same old stuff."

I laughed a little because *stuff* was what Holden and I had taken to calling our crotch areas. As in: *You ain't never gonna find a home for that stuff.* Or: *Don't be bringing that stuff round here, less you aims to use it, Mr. Rooster.* We were dorks. This is how dorks in our town talked.

Astrid stepped out of the shadows. She was puffy around the eyes.

"You're lucky to be getting out," she said. "Heading off somewhere real."

"What happened? Was it something at the party?"

She took a breath and straightened up, tucked a loose strand of hair behind her ear. "Nothing I couldn't have predicted a month ago. Walk me home, okay Tommy?"

I don't know that I can express the extent to which I welcomed this invitation. My body made all sorts of little yips. It felt good to be taken into confidence, to play a supporting role. I wanted that to be the extent of my interest. But, of course, I was also hoping. Any guy who tells you otherwise is full of shit.

"Sure," I said. "Yeah."

"I'm no idiot," Astrid said. "I knew Milikan was a sketcher." That was the word we used for guys who slept around a lot, whereas girls in our town who did that were called *skeez.* "I figured it might be a one-night thing. But he didn't need to play me. He didn't need to tell me how he was so happy to be with me and wasn't this special and he'd been waiting for months."

"He said that?"

"Yeah, he said a lot of crap. A real sketcher. A real sketch *artiste.*" Astrid laughed, sadly. "And, you know, you always wait for the phone call. I mean, we had a great time. That's the worst part."

A great time. I pondered those words, what they implied in terms of limbs and leverage and sweat. I ached to be the subject of such a statement.

"I knew he might not call, okay? But there was no need for him to show up with Little Miss Perky Tits. I mean, he knew all my friends were going to be there."

"He showed up with her and everything?"

"They were macking the whole time. God, I hate that little bitch." Astrid looked surprised she'd actually said this. Immediately her tone softened. "It's not her fault. Whatever. Scott doesn't like me because I'm not a little sporty girl."

"What about volleyball?"

"Volleyball doesn't make you a sporty girl."

She was right. This was, in its own way, a kind of variation on the beauty gradient. There were people who had bodies that looked as if they played sports and people who didn't and often it was irrelevant, especially in the case of girls, whether you actually played sports or not. The cheerleaders, for instance, who wouldn't be caught dead chucking a softball, all had sporty bods. It was a matter of appearances. And there was no middle ground, not in high school, not in a town like Nashua. I didn't have a sporty body, even though I played soccer and badminton. I looked like "a fence post with arms," as Holden's real dad put it after one of my long-ago physicals.

"I knew he was a sketcher," Astrid murmured. "But I would've liked to have fooled around with him again." She shook her head. "Hey, you should maybe go back and see about the philosopher."

"Why?"

"He was getting pretty wasted."

"He can take care of himself," I said.

We were near Astrid's house. I felt a gnawing desire to touch her, to touch her there under the flickering streetlamp, the faint moon. I knew the circumstances were all wrong, that she was heartbroken over this jerk, and that any affection thrown my way was going to be of the incidental, compromised, rebound type. And I didn't care.

I felt I deserved Astrid. I worked hard in school, and during the summers. I worked hard at listening to people, and helping them, and I had a mom who was difficult to live with, crazy, and this craziness carried a kind of taint that I had to battle against all the time, to convince everyone, myself included, that I was just a normal kid, maybe a little goofy, but normal.

"The guy's a jerk," I said. "Milikan. He doesn't know a good thing when he sees it. Really. He's making a big mistake."

"You're sweet," she said.

"Really. He acts like he's God's gift. You should hear the way he talks."

This was a mistake. Astrid's eyes sharpened. "What does he say?"

"Oh, you know. Just the standard bullshit."

"Does he talk about the girls he's scammed on?"

"No," I said quickly. "Nothing like that. He talks about other guys' girlfriends, how a particular girl looked at a party. Shit like that."

Astrid seemed relieved and then, in the space of a sigh, simply tired of worrying the situation. She was a big, cheerful girl and some of that cheer was obviously in place as a way of holding dark feelings at bay.

"Hey," she said, "when're you heading out?"

"Beginning of September."

"Psyched?"

"Yeah, I guess. It'll be good to get out of Nashua."

We were right in front of Astrid's house, a house I used to pass every day on my way back from grade school. It was a green colonial, two stories high. I'd been inside a couple of times, for parties. Her father was a dentist and her mother was a big shot in the PTA who made unbelievably good cupcakes. When I was a little kid I imagined it would be nice to have Astrid as a girlfriend because I could have those cupcakes whenever I liked. My mom didn't bake.

"I'm jealous," Astrid said, and sighed. "I'd like to get out of this whole county."

"State'll be cool," I said. "I mean, there'll be plenty of people you know."

"That's the problem," she said. "Everywhere I go around here I already know everybody."

"Just think of it as an option," I said. "You can hang out with them, if you want. But they'll be plenty of new people."

"Right," she announced. "The best way to be a grown-up is to be a grown-up."

I was hoping for an invitation to come inside, or at least sit on her porch. She might want some company, and we could shoot the breeze in the way grown-ups do, talking into the night, having some wine and cheese, maybe. Sophisticated food. And then, when the time came, one or the other of us would make a very sophisticated reference to getting ready for bed, and we would go about our business like nothing special was going to happen, just two grown-ups getting ready to have consensual intercourse.

"Listen, Tommy, thanks for walking me home. You're the best. Really. You should go see about the philosopher." Astrid gave me a quick hug and I looked into her round face for something, anything, beyond friendship. Her lipstick was crumbling at the edges.

The quick hug was the worst, most deadly sign of friendship. It showed just how little physical contact could mean. Even cold shoulders were better than quick hugs, Holden maintained, because they at least signified some sort of tension.

I was sure Valentino never got a quick hug.

There wasn't much left of the party by the time I arrived. A few couples were lumbering to some old Lionel Richie song. Liz Wheaton herself was in tears for some reason and her friends were huddled around her. The keg was suds. A snub-nosed little blond who had once kissed Holden at a junior high dance and never forgiven him looked up when I opened the gate. "If it isn't the fucking Good Humor man," she said.

I stood there on that lawn and stared at the drunk dancing couples and the few guys picking at chips and felt an intense need to be free of it all. It was like Astrid said: everywhere I went, I knew everybody, and they knew me. I was the sweet, skinny kid who scooped ice cream in a smudged white shirt, who got put into soccer games at the end, when it no longer mattered.

I was happy to see Holden's car in front of my house. He could tell me what happened at the party, at least. I put my bike away and slipped in through the garage door. I didn't like to make too much noise because my mom was a light sleeper. Anything you did might wake her up.

I flicked on the light in my room but Holden wasn't there. Then I heard a door close down the hall. I bumped right into him in the hallway.

"Hey dude," he said. His shirt was unbuttoned and he stunk of beer.

"What's going on?" I said.

"Nothing," Holden said. "I decided to crash over here, thas all. Too lit to drive home."

"Who let you in?"

"Your ma."

I didn't like the way Holden kept angling his face away.

"Were you in there?" I pointed to my mom's room.

"Shit, dude. Lemme take a piss." Holden ducked into the bathroom. I reached for the doorknob but Holden held it shut. "I'll be out inna sec," he said. "Just hold on."

I knocked on my mom's door, but there was no answer. Holden took what sounded like the world's longest piss. Finally, he appeared in the doorway.

He held up his hands, like the light from my desk lamp was hurting him. Then I saw that one eye was all red and swollen. His lip was swollen too.

"Fuck, dude, what happened?"

Holden touched his lip. "You ever been punched? Man, gettin' punched sucks."

"Who punched you?"

"Aw shit. My head really hurts. I wanna go sleep. Lemme go sleep." He leaned into my room and slumped against the wall and slid down, until he sat with his head between his knees.

"He hit you, didn't he?"

Holden stayed where he was and waved his arm a bit. I could see that his knuckles were bruised, and I hoped that meant he'd gotten in a few shots of his own.

"Yeah," Holden said quietly.

"Why'd he hit you?"

Holden's head, with all its shaggy hair, bobbed a bit. Then it stopped. "I was lit," he said. "Whatever. I talked back. I told him what I really thought. Christ he hits hard."

"Did you call the cops? The cops could arrest him for hitting a minor."

"No. No cops."

"So that's why you came back here? You were talking with my mom?"

"Yeah," Holden said. His head began bobbing again and I could hear wet breath rattling through his nose. From down the hall, I heard my mother start wailing. Then Holden began crying too.

There are moments when life requires you to rise to the occasion of some deep, otherwise irrational understanding. This is what separates friendship from acquaintance, kindness from consideration, grace from goodness, maybe, and in the sound of both of them, Holden and my mother, weeping and weeping in the small house where I had grown up, in our shitass town, on this too-warm July night, with snot dripping from Holden's nose onto his bloodstained shirt, I saw how desperate he was. The feeling of a life going nowhere, of being an enemy in his own home, of having no place to put his thoughts or feelings except into sad, overblown theories, his desire to replace one mother for another, and, in a moment of weakness, his desire to touch and be touched, and all the anger, and how all these feelings might make him want to do something taboo and full of betrayal. I understood all of this. I even wanted to forgive him. But I knew also that I needed to get out of the house, needed to get away from the two of them, to clear my head.

"You're in pretty rough shape," I said. "Why don't you take the bed."

"Hey Tommy," he said. "Yer the best, man. I gotta tell you something, okay?"

"You don't have to tell me anything."

"No, lemme tell you man. Hey man."

"I'm gonna go get the fan. Go to sleep."

"No man, you listen to this, man! You're my best friend and you gotta listen." Holden was hyperventilating. I didn't know what to do. I stood in the doorway with my chest clenching and unclenching.

Holden tried to get up. He wanted to address me face to face. But his legs gave way and he hit the carpet and lay there palming his forehead. "All that stuff about Valentino," he said. "That stuff was bullshit. I made it up, okay? Valentino was born beautiful. He was a beautiful fuckin' little baby." Holden looked up for a sec. His eyes were wet and starting to blacken. "Look, your ma and me were jus talkin."

"Sure," I said. "Go to sleep."

I slipped outside and let my feet march me through the neighborhood I knew so well that even the cracks in the sidewalks seemed reminders of a history I did not want, that I was going to have to rewrite anyway. I got the idea that I wanted to see my old grade school. I did this sometimes, late at night. Or had done this, anyway, in the days after my dad left. I liked how small everything seemed, small and peaceful, the playground stuff and the murals and even the doors to the classrooms.

The lights were out at Astrid's house, but I walked over to the window I was pretty sure was hers and knocked. I tried to imagine what it was like inside her room, what it smelled like and where the bed was, and what the sheets felt like. I saw a light flick on and after a minute a hand cleared the curtain away. For a second I thought I'd fucked up, because the face hovering behind the pane looked saggy and webbed. Then I saw the volleyball T-shirt and realized it was Astrid after all, only that she was tired.

When she saw me her shoulders fell a bit. She cranked open the window. "Tommy. What are you doing?"

"Hey," I said. "I'm heading over to Palmer. You know, to the playground, to hang out. It's quiet over there, and I thought, you know, you might want to come."

The lamp behind her was shining through her T-shirt. I could see the outline of her chest, each breast swelling over her ribs, and I guess I must have been staring because she went and got a robe and came back and sat on the sill. "It's late, Tommy." She yawned. "I was sleeping."

"Yeah, I'm sorry."

She yawned again. I worried she was going to ask me to leave.

"You're going to Palmer?" she said. "Why're you going there?" She peered at me more carefully now. "What's going on, Tommy?"

"Nothing," I said. "I just wanted to talk."

Astrid played with the belt on her robe, ran it between two fingers, let it fall. "Do we have to go to Palmer?" she said. "It's creepy over there. I don't like the apartments near there. Just come around to the porch."

"Sure," I said. "Cool."

"Shhhh. Quiet down, Tommy. If my dad hears you, he'll kill me."

"Sorry. Sorry."

I went around and sat on the porch swing, and thought about the last time I had been on that porch, which was five years ago, at a big Memorial Day picnic. My mom had her hair piled on top of her head, and a summer dress, and fresh lipstick every time she turned around. All the girls from my year in school were there, and Holden in his sad little leisure suit. I watched my mother lean over the table to serve potato salad. Her arm moved like a swan's neck and her lips were the wings of butterflies and I can see now that it took a lot of effort for her to look as put together as she did. It was days like that, I guess, that kept my dad around a couple more years.

But now Astrid was padding toward the door and I looked down and arranged myself, sort of puffed my crotch and finger-combed my hair. Astrid had her robe on and a baseball cap. She looked around and then sat down on the wicker chair across from me.

"What's going on?" she whispered. "You're acting weird, Tommy."

"Weird?"

"Knocking on my window like that. You nearly broke the glass."

"I just wanted to make sure you were okay. You were so upset before."

"And this thing of going over to Palmer? What kind of crazy thing is that to do?"

I was glad Astrid hadn't turned on any lights, because the way she said this rattled me. Her tone reminded me of my dad during his visits, the way he questioned me, as if frisking my heart for sorrow. What I'd envisioned when I woke Astrid was this romantic scene which would involve her realizing that she loved me, or at least liked me enough to take off her clothes. And also, later, afterward, that she would understand me, that I might be able to put my head in her lap and explain some of the things that had happened and the feelings I was having.

But now it was going the other direction and I was having to realize that I'd had all these crazy desires, and that they were just that:

crazy. That rather than being rescued by the love of Astrid Miller, I was actually exposing myself in a foolish way, and this was dangerous. I felt like I might start bawling. "I was just worried about you," I said quietly. "You know, you're usually a pretty happy person, a strong person, and I wanted to make sure you were okay, that's all."

"I'm fine," she said. I could tell she wanted to say something more, to maybe defend herself from so much caretaking. But what she said was this: "How's your mom?"

I don't know how much she knew about my home situation, but she must have known some because her dad worked at the clinic where my mom got her medication.

I said nothing.

"I used to think about your mom," she said. "She is such a beautiful woman. Is she all right, Tommy? Is that what this is about?"

I felt something shutter up inside me and shook my head and tried to laugh. "No. It's like I told you, I just wanted to talk. No big deal."

Astrid nodded.

I tried to make my mind go blank, and when that didn't work I heard myself say, "Listen, Ast, I just wanted to tell you a story. That's the truth. As I was walking back to my house I was thinking about this story I heard recently. About Valentino. Rudolph Valentino."

"The old movie star?"

"Yeah." I swallowed, and waited for my voice to firm up. "Do you know anything about Valentino?"

It was a warm night in Nashua and the crickets were sawing away on their legs, and I could see, for a moment, that I was going to leave it all behind, that I didn't have much longer, and that made the night, with its dark air and failed moon, almost beautiful. And then Astrid did something that was also quite beautiful, something that probably saved my life, in the sense that I could keep it in my memory forever, and return to it, and let it stand against everything else that seemed so awfully true at that moment.

She loosened the strap of her robe and pulled it open a bit and fanned herself, and I could see the tops of her breasts there, rising from the white of her chest. And she nodded at me, nodded me forward, and I saw from her expression that this was like a gift she was giving me, a final gift, and I got up slowly and knelt down before her. And she closed her eyes and took my head in her hands and moved me against her skin, which was warm and smooth and smelled like lotion. And she said, "Tell me." And I said, "Tell you what?" And she said, "Tell me what you were going to tell me. Tell me about Valentino."

How to Love
a Republican

I met Darcy Hicks early in the primary season, at a dive in Randolph, New Hampshire. She was sitting at the bar in a blue skirt, sipping from a tumbler and looking bored. The locals had hit on her already. But they were missing it. Her edges were too crisp for the room. Her makeup was nearly invisible.

The stool next to her opened up and I sat down. A Kenny Loggins tune came on the jukebox and the bartender began to sing along. Darcy glanced at her drink, trying to decide whether another would make matters better or worse. I'd had a miserable day and was feeling sorry for myself, lonely, a little reckless. I introduced myself and asked her please not to take offense if I bought her a drink.

Darcy turned slowly. In profile she had seemed dangerously icy. But straight on her face was sweet and a little flushed.

"Jack and ginger," she said.

I ordered two.

It turned out we were both in New Hampshire doing issue work. Darcy was pitching agricultural subsidies to the Republicans; I was pitching drug counseling to the Dems. I'd spent the past week trolling rehab centers, listening to earnest social workers and sad, unconvincing ex-junkies. At night, I squeezed into the tiny hotel bathtub and tried to wash the smoke out of my pores. Darcy was faring no better. She'd twisted her ankle that morning touring a derelict strawberry farm.

"Who farms here?" she said. "What would they farm, granite?"

"Maybe they thought they'd sent you to Vermont."

She shook her head. "There are no Republicans in Vermont."

The truth is, we were on the fringes of the campaign, miles from the action; our duties were more ceremonial than anything. But there was in each of us the bug of politics, a talky competitiveness, a desire to impose our sense of right on the world. We carried, along with our clattery Beltway cynicism and our Motorolas, a tremendous vulnerability to hope. And now, as we talked and drank, this vulnerability became shared property, like the pack of Camel Lights that lay between us, or the tales of Model UN coups, the geeky adolescent versions of our adult passion.

Outside, the December night was crisp. A fog had rolled in and lay draped over the pine barrens like gauze. We stood beside my rental car, shivering, swinging a little. Darcy was packed neatly into her blue cotton blend. Her hair was the color of wet straw and fell to her clavicle. A flower belonged behind her ear. Kissing her seemed the most uncomplicated decision I had made in years.

So there was that, an evening of esprit de corps, some very fine necking in the great hither and yon of the electorate. Back in D.C., the situation was a little less clear.

Darcy worked at the Fund For Tradition, a think tank devoted to—as the swanky, four-color pamphlets told it—*fiscal restraint and the defense of traditional values.* I was at Citizen Action, a relic of the LBJ era. We didn't have pamphlets. Our mission was to lobby the halls of power on behalf of the disenfranchised. To piss, in other words, up the mighty tree of capitalism.

We conducted the same basic life at a slightly different amplitude. The brutal hours of apprenticeship, the hasty lunches and reports whose sober facts gummed our thoughts. We were both involved with other people, people more like ourselves, who satisfied us in a placid way. I might never have seen her again. Except that I did.

She was standing alone in the Senate gallery. Congress was on break, the tourists gone. Darcy gazed down into the darkening well of the Senate. She was wearing a peacoat and a dark pillbox hat, which now, in my memory, I have affixed with a veil, though I'm certain this was not the case.

I circled the gallery and waited for her to notice me. When I called her name, she gasped and placed a hand over her heart.

"Oh Billy! It's you."

"I'm sorry. Did I startle you?"

"No," she said. "Not at all."

"You look beautiful," I said.

This wasn't what I'd meant to say. It was certainly too ardent for the setting. But it was the truest thing I was feeling, and anyway Darcy had this effect on me.

She shook her head a little, then blushed. "What are you doing here?" she said.

"I'm not sure. I was visiting a friend downstairs, a guy who works with Sarbanes. I just sort of wandered up here."

"I come here all the time," Darcy said. "It helps me think."

"About what?"

She pursed her lips. "Why we're here, I guess. The desire to effect good in an arena of civility."

"Is that Jefferson?"

"Not really. It's me."

The smell of the Senate rose from the empty well, old leather and something vaguely peppery, Brylcreem maybe. The place exuded a sense of quiet dignity, which was more than the absence of its usual clamor, seemed closer, in the end, to the calm we hoped to find at the center of our lives.

"Does that sound hokey, Billy?" Darcy said suddenly.

"Not at all."

"You don't think so?" Her face leapt from the dark fabric of her coat, sweetly arrayed in worry.

"Are you hungry?" I said.

Darcy opened her mouth but said nothing.

"Other plans?"

"Sort of. I should . . ." She looked at me for a moment. "Hold on."

"If you've got plans, I don't want to impose."

Darcy laughed, a bit lavishly. "I wouldn't let you impose," she said, and drew the cell phone from her coat pocket.

There are so many competing interests on the human heart. For those of us truly terrified of death, intent on leaving some kind of mark, plowing through our impatient twenties with an *agenda*, there are moments when chemistry—the chemistry between bodies, the chemistry of connection—seems no more than a sentimental figment. And then something happens, you meet a woman and you can't stop looking at her mouth. Everything she does, every word and gesture, stirs inside you, strikes the happy gong. The way she throws herself into a fresh field of snow. The delicacy of her sneezes, like a candle being snuffed. The sugary sting of whiskey on her tongue. Chemistry in its sensual aspects. Chemistry the ultimate single-issue voter.

We were both tipsy and tangled in my flannel sheets. We'd talked about not letting this happen, this sudden rush into the secret bodies. But Darcy, her neck, the length of her torso, the wisp of corn silk above her pelvic basin, and the gentle application of her hands, her generous, unfeigned devotions to my body—which I secretly loathed, which shamed me for its deficiencies of grace and muscle—and her hair reeling across my chest. . . . All these came at me in a tumble of violent emotion, stripped from me the language with which one crafts cautious deferrals, the *maybe I should go*, the sudden pause, the stuttered breath and step back, the gallant bonered retreat to the bathroom.

No. We made instead a ridiculous flying machine in two clamped parts. In the thick of our clumsy desire, pungent and shameless, we clutched one another by the cheeks, let the skin of our bellies smack briskly, and flew.

"So that's what it's like to love a Republican," I said.

"There are other ways, too." Darcy giggled. "Do you have cigarettes? I'd kill for a cigarette."

I reached into my bedside drawer.

"Why do we hide them?"

"They're an ugly habit."

She took a slow drag and blew the smoke at the ceiling. "Oh yeah."

Outside a light snow fell. The cars on the road made a sound like the surf. The moon lit Darcy's face. Her nose was a little blunt. One of her incisors pushed out dramatically from the neat band of her teeth. These flaws served to particularize her beauty. One's memory snagged on them.

"You're my first beard," she said thoughtfully.

"How was it?"

"Bristly."

"Like being with a lumberjack?"

"A lumberjack wouldn't whimper."

"Did I whimper?"

"Unless that was me."

Darcy sat up and peered around the room. Che Guevara stared down at her from the closet door, in his fierce mustache. My fertility goddesses stood ranked along the sill, squat figures with sagging breasts and hips round as swales. I waited for Darcy to ask me about them so I could recite my Peace Corps stories. (I'd saved a little girl's life! A goat had been killed in my honor!) But she only took another drag and covered her warm little breasts.

"Where are we again?"

"My apartment."

"The address, you dope."

"Why do you want the address?"

"For the cab."

"Oh please don't go. I'd rather if you stayed. Or I could drive you."

"No. I need to think about this."

"Can't we think together? I'd like to think with you."

"I'm not sure you're the best thing for my thought process."

Darcy rose from the bed and began collecting her clothes. I watched her move around the room. I wanted terribly for her to come close enough that I could take a bite of her tush, which trembled like a pale bell. But this was not going to happen. From the other room came the slithery sound of panty hose, the clasp of a bra.

"What's there to think about?" I called out. "Was this a mistake? Because I don't feel like this was a mistake."

Darcy reemerged looking combed and dangerous, like something from a winter catalogue. She took a last drag off her cigarette and dropped it in her wineglass. A horn sounded below, in the street.

"Can I at least walk you down?"

"You're sweet. I wish you wouldn't." She set her fingers to her throat and said, a little dreamily, "I'm going to have a rash tomorrow, from your beard."

I went to the window and watched her slip into the cab. There was something tragically illicit about the moment. I didn't know what to do. The golden thread between us had snapped. How had this happened? I threw open the window and bellowed: "Why do I feel like I've been taken advantage of?"

Darcy looked up. Her face shone behind the dark pane. Just before she laughed, her mouth pulled down slightly at the corners, which suggested, even in the midst of her gaiety, an irrevocable sadness. I was certain, gazing down through the soft tiers of snow, the smell of her rising up from my beard, that this sadness could be undone. This was my bright idea. I was, after all, a good liberal.

But then Darcy disappeared and I was left to moon liberally through the long white weekend, during which I spoke and ate and fucked dispiritedly with the woman I was dating, a good woman, with earnest rings of hair and a powerful devotion to social justice.

I called Darcy at the office and listened to her outgoing message, whose crisp, chirpy tones made me feel renounced, and left two excruciatingly casual messages, and took lunch at the bistro across from the Fund For Tradition, and one afternoon wandered over to Capitol Hill and kneeled in the cool Senate gallery, waiting like a parishioner. By week two my heart had dithered into a boyish panic. I left a final message on her machine telling her that I didn't understand what was going on but that I was hurt and confused and felt that something had been betrayed, the feelings that had passed between us, that these feelings felt real to me and that they didn't come along very often and shouldn't be squandered, and that if she felt any of these same things, even unsteadily, she owed it to herself, as well as just to common decency, to call me back, that dodging me was no solution, unless she was one of those people who offered intimacy and then withdrew, who, for lack of a better word, *used* people, in which case she was best not to call back at all. But that, if she was still, if she felt, even a little, I was sorry to sound petulant, I didn't mean to, but I was upset and if could she please call me back and here was my number, at which point a voice came on the line noting that my three minutes were up and would I like to leave the message, or re-record it, or erase the whole thing, which I did.

What was this thing between us, anyway? Just some Jungle Fever of the low political stripe. Who was Darcy Hicks, anyway? Maybe this was her secret fetish: sexing up the left and reporting the details back to her Republican overlords. On and on I went, the florid improvisations of the wounded heart.

And then, just as this clatter was subsiding, I saw her again. On C-SPAN. She stood at the edge of the frame as John McCain—fresh off his win in New Hampshire—rallied the troops in an Iowa VFW hall. Darcy kept drifting in and out of the picture. She was wearing a red dress and smiling desperately. McCain told the crowd he'd come to Elk Horn for one purpose: to discuss the plight of the small family farm, and the need for renewed agricultural subsidies.

The phone rang. It was late, one in the morning on a Tuesday.

"What's your address again?" Darcy said.

I wanted to say something caustic and clever but adrenaline had flushed my chest and all the words I had marshaled in my rehearsals for this moment seemed stingy and beside the point.

The line crackled. "Billy? Hurry up! My battery's going dead."

"Where are you?"

"That's what I'm asking you. Oh!" Darcy squealed, and there was a thump. Her phone began to cut out, so that I could hear her voice only in snatches, urgent little phonemes: *time, get, numb*——. The line went dead.

Twenty minutes later my buzzer rang. Darcy burst into my apartment. She was flushed, her lipstick was off-kilter. A purple fleece hat sat goofily on her head. She threw her arms around me and burrowed her cold cheeks into my neck. A noise of pleasure came from her throat, as if she were settling into a hot bath.

"Aren't you glad to see me?" she murmured.

I stood there trying not to relent.

"I'm just back in town," Darcy went on. "I was in Iowa. Trent sent me out on subsidies and ethanol production, and John, John McCain, he used one of my workups in his stump. And then he asked me—or Roger, his press guy—asked me to do advance work in South Carolina! Can you believe it? You have to meet John in person to get the whole picture. But those five years in Vietnam, I mean, he just cuts through all the bullshit. The man radiates charisma."

I found myself (rather unattractively) wishing to torture Senator John McCain.

Darcy pulled her hat off and her hair fell in a tangle.

"Are you proud of me?" she said.

"I'm a little confused actually."

"It's a confusing time," Darcy said breezily. "Election years always are. Aren't you going to kiss me? I know you're glad to see me." She nodded ever so slightly at my erection.

I tried to look indignant. "I left messages for you."

"I know I should have called. I'm sorry. Don't be mad at me. There was a lot going on. Not just Iowa. There were other things." She slipped her hands inside my pajamas and touched my ribs. "Are you cold, baby? You've got goose bumps. Can we lie down? I'm so tired. I've been thinking about lying down with you."

I was sore with the need for Darcy. She smelled of lilacs and gin; her body pressed forward. But I didn't like the way I'd been feeling, and I distrusted this erotic lobbying.

"What other things?" I said.

"I'm a loyal person. What I've been doing has been for us, okay? Just trust me, Billy. Don't you want to trust me?"

"Yeah. I mean, I want—"

"Then do. Just do. Quit asking questions and kiss me."

"I just want to know what we are."

Darcy let out a little shriek of frustration. "Would you stop being so *literal?* This is a love affair, Billy. Okay? Withstand a little doubt. I'm the one who's taking the risk here."

"Meaning what?"

"Stop being naive. The woman always loses power in a sexual relationship."

"Not always," I said.

Darcy sighed. She took her hands off me and stepped back. "I just flew four hours with a goddamn baby howling in my ear. I haven't slept more than three hours in the past two days. I'm expected to show up to work tomorrow, bright and early, to host a reception for Jack Fucking Kemp. I don't do this. I don't come over to men's houses. But I'm here, Billy. Do you understand? I am here. Now take me in your arms and *do something*, or I'm going home right now."

What Darcy enjoyed most was a good lathering between the thighs. As a lifelong liberal, this was one of my specialties. In some obscure but plausible fashion, I viewed the general neglect of the region as a bedrock of conservatism. The female sex was, in political terms, the equivalent of the inner city: a dark and mysterious zone, vilified by the powerful, derided as incapable of self-improvement, entrenched and smelly. Going down on a woman was a dirty business, humiliating, potentially infectious, best delegated to the sensitivos of the Left.

I relished the act, which I considered to be what Joe Lieberman would have termed, in his phlegmy rabbinical tone, a *mitzvah*. It required certain sacrifices. The deprivation of oxygen, to begin with. A certain ridiculousness of posture; cramping in the lower extremities. One had to engage with the process. There were no quick fixes.

This was especially true in Darcy's case. She was scandalized by the intensity of her desire, and highly aroused by this scandal. But the going was slow. If I told her "I want to kiss you there" she would grow flustered and glance about helplessly. Just act, was her point. Ditch all the soppy acknowledgment, the naming of things in the dark. The word *pussy* made her wince. (A tainted word, I admit, but one I employed with utmost fondness and in the spirit of fond excitements.)

I kissed my way down her body—the damp undersides of her breasts, her bumpy sternum, the belly she lamented not ridding herself of. Always, I could feel the tendons of her groin tensing. I nipped at them occasionally.

She perfumed herself elaborately, which meant withstanding an initial astringency, after which she tasted wonderfully, meaning strongly of herself, the brackish bouquet of her insides. I was careful not to linger in any one spot but to explore the entire intricate topography, the nerves flushed with blood and tingling mysteriously, while Darcy pressed herself back on the pillows and turned to face the wall and murmured the blessed nonsensical approvals of climax.

The body releases its electricity, merges with another, and together there is something like God in this pleasure. But afterward, in the quiet redolent air, there must also be offerings of truth. And so the mystery of love deepens.

Darcy's given name was Darlene. She'd grown up in Ashton, Pennsylvania, a rural township south of Allentown. Her grandpas had been farmers. Then the world had changed, grown more expensive and mechanical, and somehow less reliable. So her father, rather than inheriting dark fields of barley, worked for Archer Daniels Midland. (Her mother, it went without saying, was a homemaker.) All three of her sisters and her brother still lived in Ashton. She was an aunt eight times.

Darcy recognized that she was different from her family. But she was reluctant to speak too pointedly about these differences.

Instead, she turned the Hicks clan into a comedy routine, delivering updates in the flat accent of her grandpa Tuck.

Signs of her double life abounded. She dressed in Ann Taylor, but used a crock pot. She stored her birth-control pills in a bedside drawer, beside the worn green Bible she had been given in Sunday school. Her mantle displayed photos of the grip-and-grin with Arlen Specter, Robert Bork, Newt Gingrich. Only in the shadowed corner of her bedroom did one see a young, toothy Darcy, resplendent in acid wash and pink leg warmers, smiling from the seat of an old tractor on Grandpa Tuck's homestead. The photo was taken just before he sold the final acres to a chemical plant, back in '89.

As for me, I'd grown up outside Hartford. My parents had marched for Civil Rights and protested the war. Then they had kids, moved to a leafy suburb, and renovated an old Victorian. Their domestic and professional duties tired them out, left them susceptible to bourgeois enjoyments. But the way I remembered them—needed to remember them—was as young, beautiful radicals.

What we wanted from politics, in the end, was what we had been deprived by our families. I hoped to create a world in which justice and compassion would be the enduring measure. Darcy sought permission to expand her horizons, to experience her prosperity without guilt. We both held to the notion that it mattered who won office and how they governed. Nothing, in the end, mattered more.

Yet it never would have occurred to us, not in a million years, that the 2000 election would turn volatile. The presidential candidates were a couple of second-raters, awkwardly hawking the same square yard of space, at the corner of Main and Centrist.

*   *   *

And so we lay about on weekends, scattering sheafs of newsprint onto the sunny hardwood floors of my apartment, lamenting (silently, to ourselves) the hopeless bias of the *Post* and *Times*, tumbling the stately avenues of downtown, drowning in happy wine and letting our messages stack up.

We were both too hooked on politics to ignore the subject entirely. But we had to be careful not to push too far into ideology. Darcy was altogether suspicious of the word. "Just a fancy way of saying policy aims," she insisted.

I disagreed. To me, the Left was a living force, animated by heroic and martyred ideas: Civil Rights. The War on Poverty. Christ Himself—as I argued in an unreadably earnest undergraduate paper—was a classic New Deal Democrat. Darcy listened to my ravings with a polite purse of her lips. She viewed me as quaint, I think.

But Darcy had her own dewy allegiances. Reagan, for instance. They'd named an airport after him. Now he had Alzheimer's and the news told stories of his decay, over which Darcy clucked. "He made it acceptable to love this country again," she told me. "Don't give me that snotty look, Billy. He was an American hero."

This was astounding to me: Ronald Reagan! The man who had allowed Big Business to run the country, slashed social programs, gorged the national debt on wacko military systems, funneled arms to Nicaraguan murderers, and just generally sodomized Mother Nature.

So, in other words, we learned to avoid policy aims.

By March Darcy was traveling nearly every week. She was unofficially on loan to the McCain campaign, which was full of reformist spunk but foundering in the polls. I expected Darcy to be devastated by the results of Super Tuesday, which all but assured Bush the nomination. But she emerged from her flight (a red-eye out of Atlanta) beaming.

"Kenny O'Brien talked to Roger about me. He wants me to do advance work for Dubya! Isn't that *amazing!*"

My reaction to this news was complicated. I was thrilled and impressed. Darcy was making a name for herself. But this would mean more travel for her, more prestige, more action. While I remained in D.C., plinking out obscure proposals on how to reduce recidivism, stewing over whether to vote for the Android or the Spoiler. And missing her.

Beyond envy, I felt genuinely unsettled. Darcy had been a rabid McCain supporter—one of his true believers. She had derided Bush as a semipro, a lollygagger. It was hard for me to fathom how she could now throw her support behind him.

"We fought the good fight," Darcy assured me. "The key is that we managed to push finance reform onto the agenda."

"You really think Shrub is going to do anything on that?" I said. "The guy raised fifty million before he even announced."

Darcy frowned. "Don't be so cynical," she said. "Have a little faith for a change. Oh, I'm hungry, Billy. Where can we get a burger at this hour?"

Winter limped into April and we barely noticed. The dirty slush glittered and the gutters lay ripe with magic. In early May the cherry blossoms reemerged along Pennsylvania and I turned twenty-seven. Darcy organized a celebration at a tapas bar in Foxhall Road, one of those places where the waiters are obliged to enforce a spirit of merriment by squirting rioja from boda bags into the mouths of particularly valued diners. Darcy, in her little cocktail dress, offered a toast, while my friends glanced in horror at the table beside us, where a pack of trashed dot-commers were plying the waitress to flash her tits.

Darcy considered the evening a triumph, and I hoped she was right. My friends were a glum and brainy lot, nonprofit warriors and outreach workers. They could see how smitten I was and spoke to Darcy with elaborate courtesy. But to them she must have appeared no different from the hundreds of other GOP tootsies cruising the capital in their jaunty hair ribbons.

I met Darcy's friends the following week, at a luncheon held in the executive dining room, on the second floor of the Fund's stately colonial. The maître d' grimaced politely at my sweater. He whisked into the cloakroom and reappeared with an elegant camel's hair sports coat.

Darcy waved to me and smiled, which instantly snuffed my doubt, made me hum a silent pledge of allegiance to our love. The men at her table wore matching dark green blazers, with an FFT in gold script over the breast pocket. Darcy stood out like a rose in a stand of rhododendron.

The servers were brisk Europeans, officious in their table-side preparation of chateaubriand. George F. Will delivered the keynote, wearily lamenting the "deracination of moral authority" to general mirth and light applause, though his platitudes were obscured by the sandblasting from next door, where workers were empaneling a new marble patio at the Saudi embassy.

I cannot remember the names of Darcy's colleagues, only that they seemed to have been cut from the same hearty block of wood. The older fellows evinced the serenity characteristic of a life spent in private clubs. The young guys imitated these manners. They were

clean-shaven, deeply committed carnivores who seemed, in conver-
sational lulls, to be searching the rich wainscoting for signs of a crew
oar they might take up.

They all adored Darcy, that much was obvious, and chaffed
her with careful paternalism.

"A remarkable young woman," said the gentleman on my left,
the moment she had excused herself to the bathroom. "You are
watching a future congressman from Pennsylvania."

"Congresswoman," I said, half to myself.

"Yes," he answered, poking at a rind of fat on his plate. "Darcy
mentioned that about you."

At the brief reception after lunch, while the higher-ups clus-
tered about Will, Darcy introduced me to her mentor. Trent was a
thick blond fellow with the most marvelous teeth I had ever seen.
"This your special friend, Hicks?" Trent said. "Good to meet you."

"Bill," I said.

"Bill. Good to meet you, Bill."

He gripped my hand and held it for a few beats. It occurred to
me that Trent had served in the Armed Forces, possibly all four of
them.

"Darcy tells me you've done some work for Bradley."

"Not really. A little volunteering."

"A good man," Trent said. "Principled. Shame he got ambushed by Gore. Not surprising, especially, but a shame. What're
your plans for the election, Bill?"

"I'll probably be sitting this one out," I said.

Trent barked. "How long you been in the District, Bill? No
such thing." He winked and drew Darcy against him. "You watch
this one, Bill. She's going places."

Darcy blushed.

"You take care of her," Trent said.

"Darcy does a pretty good job of taking care of herself."

Trent dragged his knuckles across his chin and shot me a look of such naked disdain that I took a step backward. Then he wrapped Darcy in a bear hug, kissed her on the brow, and wished me well.

"He just seemed a little aggressive," I said to Darcy later, in her office.

"Nonsense. He's just protective."

"You know him better than me."

"Wait a second." Darcy's eyes—they were steel blue—flickered with her triumph. "You're jealous!"

"The guy was all over you, honey. And the way he behaved toward me—"

"He wasn't all over me. He was being *affectionate.*"

"Is that what they're calling it these days?"

Darcy began to laugh. She'd had three cups of punch and was still flying. I listened to her gleeful hiccups and watched the chandelier in the foyer glint. "Trent's LC," she said finally. "Log Cabin, Billy. He's gay."

She began laughing again.

Trent the Gay Republican? "He must be thrilled with Shrub's support of the sodomy laws in Texas."

"There you go again," Darcy said. She was imitating Reagan now. "Judging people. I thought you enlightened liberals didn't judge people."

Darcy traveled throughout spring and into summer, and this lent our relations an infatuated rhythm. My heart beat wildly as I waited for her plane to land. This was not her beauty acting upon me, the glamour of her ambitions, even the promise of sex, but the sense of good intention she radiated, a kindheartedness measured in the drowsy hours before she could assemble her public self. This was my favorite time: Darcy in the shades of dawn, warm with sleep, her hair scattered across the pillow.

There was an ease to her domestic rituals, the way she snipped coupons (which she would never use) and scrubbed her lonely appliances and listened sympathetically to the latest reports from Ashton. She fretted endlessly over what to pack for her trips. "I'm too fat for these slacks," she complained. "I'm one big, fat ass, Billy."

This was not true. If anything, Darcy was growing slimmer. But these sudden bouts of self-doubt were necessary to her maintenance. They were vestiges of her girlhood, of the awkward striver who lived behind the awesome machinery of her charm. They were the part of her that needed me.

I was a fool to watch the Republican Convention. But there was an element of morbid curiosity at work. I wanted to see Jesse Helms reborn as an emissary of tolerance. (What would he wear? A dashiki?) And besides, I had promised Darcy. She was attending as a Bush delegate from Pennsylvania.

What has always astounded me about the Republican psyche is its capacity for shamelessness. Here was the anti-immigration party parading its little brown ones across the rostrum, the party of Family Values showcasing its finest buttoned-down catamites. Here was Big Dick Cheney—who had voted against funding Head Start as a congressman—excoriating Clinton for not doing enough to educate oppressed children. On and on it went, and nobody exploded of hypocrisy!

Darcy called me each night, giddy with the sense of how well it was coming off. "Did you see me on CNBC?" she said. "Deb Borders interviewed me. Did you see Christie Whitman, Billy? Wasn't she amazing? Okay. Don't answer that. I miss you, Billy. Do you miss me? Do you?"

"Of course I do."

"Do you love me?" she said suddenly.

"You know I do."

"Say it."

"I love you, Darcy."

And I did. It was nothing I could help.

"I love you, Billy. I love you so much."

"Where are you?" I asked. "Are you in your room?"

"I'm on my bed."

And so we progressed, deeper into our thrilling disjunction.

By October the Bush people had taken Darcy on full-time. She was living out of a suitcase, returning to D.C. with purple stains under her eyes, sleeping twelve hours straight. I took it as my duty to offer her refuge in the cause of intimacy.

And Darcy returned this devotion. Even as the campaign drew to an end, she came at me in a dizzy operatic spin, ravished for affection, for a private domain in which she could shed the careful burnishings of her ascent. One evening, as we lay flushed on gin, she announced that she had a surprise for me and rose up on her haunches and slipped off her panties and knelt back. All that remained of her pubic hair was a single delicate stripe.

I felt touched to the point of tears. Here was this miraculous creature, tuckered beyond words, right here in my apartment on the eve of the election, flashing me her vaginal mohawk. She vamped gamely even as her eyelids drooped, and licked her lovely incisor and urged me forward. How could it possibly matter that she opposed gun control?

I called Darcy at 2:42 A.M. on election night. The networks had just issued their flop on Florida and Dan Rather—in an apparent caffeine psychosis—was urging America to give Dubya a big ole Texas-sized welcome to the White House.

Darcy was across town, at the Radisson. There were whoops in the background and the echoes of a bad jazz band.

"Congratulations," I said.

"Billy! Oh, you are so sweet!"

"Well, no one likes a sore loser."

"It was so close," Darcy said. "It's a shame anyone had to lose!"

There was a rush of sound and Darcy let out a happy scream. "Stop it! Stop!" She came back on the phone. "That was Trent."

"Can you come over?" I said. "I'd like to congratulate you in person."

Darcy drew in a breath. "I'd love to. That would be so nice. But I promised some people I'd stay here. At least until Dubya gives his speech."

I was quiet for a moment.

"Honey," she said. "Are you okay? Are you mad?"

I was maybe a little mad. But I knew how hard Darcy had worked for this, how much hope she'd pinned to the outcome. She had leapt toward the thick of the race, bravely, with her arms wide and her pretty little chest exposed, while I'd thrown up my hands in disgust and voted for Nader.

"No," I said. "I'm proud of you, Darce. You deserve this."

"I love you, Billy."

"I love you too," I said quietly. "You crazy Republican bitch."

She laughed. A chorus of deep voices swelled in the background and Darcy, carried away by some shenanigans, shrieked merrily.

I wondered sometimes why she didn't just settle for some GOP bohunk with a carapace of muscles and the proper worldview. She could have had her pick. We both knew that. But that's not how the heart works. It runs to deeper needs. "I'll try to come over after the speech," Darcy whispered. "I want to see you."

Two weeks later we were in Darcy's apartment, still trying to figure out what had happened. Al Gore was on CNN, imitating someone made of flesh.

"Why doesn't he give it up?" Darcy murmured.

"Why should he give up?" I said.

"Because he lost."

We had both assumed the election would bring an end to the tension. One or the other side would win, fair and square, and we would move on.

"You can't say he lost until they count all the votes," I said. "It's just too close. Can't you see that, honey?"

Darcy sighed. She'd cut her hair into a kind of bob, which made her look a little severe. "Why did Gore ask for recounts in only four counties? He's not interested in a full and accurate count. Admit it. He wants to count until he has the votes to win."

"They both want to win. It's called a race."

"Don't patronize me, Billy."

"I wouldn't patronize you if you didn't keep oversimplifying the situation."

Darcy clicked off the TV. "Why do you talk like that, Billy? Why do you make everything so personal?"

"Trying to impeach the president for getting a blowjob? That's not *personal*? Or DeLay sending his thugs down to Miami to storm the canvassing board? What is that? Politics as usual? Are you kidding me?"

Darcy shook her head; the edges of her new haircut sawed back and forth. "I can't talk with you about this stuff. You get too angry."

"You're as pissed as I am."

"No," she said. "I just want this to be over."

We didn't say anything else, but the mists of rage hung about us. And later on, after we had retired to the bedroom, this rage hid within our desire and charged out of our bodies in a way we hoped would bring us closure. We slammed against one another and gasped and clutched, did everything we could think to enthrall the other while at the same time hoping somewhat to murder, to die together, and woke instead, in the morning, bruised and contrite.

I agreed with Darcy, after all. I wanted the election to be over. I didn't want to be angry at her, because I loved her and that love was more important than any election. I honestly *tried* to ignore the dispute. What did I care? Gore had run an awful campaign. He deserved to lose.

Gradually, though, the radical truth was coming clear: more voters had gone to the polls in Florida intending to vote for him. The statisticians understood this, and the voting-machine wonks, and even the brighter reporters, the ones who bothered to think the matter through.

The Republican strategy was to obscure this truth, to prevent at all costs a closer inspection of the ballots. In doing so, they became opponents of democracy. (There is no other way to say this.) What amazed me was the gusto with which Bush executed this treason. His fixers lied incessantly and extravagantly. His allies stormed the cameras and frothed.

Us Democrats never quite grasped that we were in a street fight. We lacked the required viciousness, the mindless loyalty. This has always been the Achilles heel of the Left: we are too fond of our own decency, too fearful of our anger. When the blackjacks come out we quit the field and call it dignity.

The cold fog of December descended on the capital and I sat in my apartment glaring at CNN, and fantasized about putting a bullet in James Baker's skull. Darcy called out to me from the answering machine, her voice loosened by red wine. My name sounded vague and hopeful in her mouth.

And then, one night, just after the final certification of votes in Florida, a knock came at the door. There was Darcy, in her blue skirt and her lovely snaggled smile. She was breathing hard. I imagined for a moment that she had run from somewhere far away, from Georgetown perhaps, through the dark banished lowlands of Prince George County, or from the tawny plains of central Pennsylvania.

"We need to talk," she said.

She fell against me, smelling of gin and lilacs and cigarettes. Here she was, this soft person, soft all the way through. I felt terribly responsible.

"Where'd you come from?"

"That bar down the street."

"The Versailles?"

"Uh-huh."

"What were you doing there?"

She looked up into my face. "My friends say I should dump you."

"What do you say?"

"I don't know. You're a good lay." She tugged at my jeans. But this was only an imitation of lust, something borrowed from the booze. Her hands soon fell away. "Where the hell have you been?"

"I haven't been anywhere. I've been here. Look, I'm sorry. I haven't quite known what to do."

"You could start by returning my calls, okay? Okay, Mr. Fucking Sensitivity?" Darcy glanced into the living room, at the pizza boxes and heaps of clothing. She shook her head. Bush was on now, staring into the camera like a frightened monkey. "Please, Billy, don't tell me you're still moping about this election."

"It's more like constructive brooding."

Darcy plopped onto the couch. Her knees pressed together and her calves flared out like jousts. This lent her an antic quality, as if she might at any moment leap to her feet and burst into a tap-dance routine. "Why are you doing this to yourself?"

"I'm not doing anything to myself."

"I just don't understand why you have to hold this against me. I don't hold your views against you."

"That's because you're winning," I muttered.

"What?"

"You're winning. You can afford the luxury of grace. But I'll tell you what, if these undervotes ever get counted and Gore pulls ahead, you and the rest—"

"That will never happen," Darcy said sharply. She smoothed her skirt with the heel of her palm and took a deep breath. "You know as well as I do that if the situation were reversed, Gore would do the same thing as Bush."

"You may be right," I said. "But if he did that, he'd be wrong. And I hope I'd have the integrity to see that."

"And I *don't* have integrity?"

"I'm not saying that. What I'm saying is . . ."

But what *was* I saying? Wasn't I saying precisely that?

Darcy narrowed her eyes and waited for me to clarify myself.

"Look, I know you have a lot invested in Bush winning. You worked hard for him. And I realize we have different views on how to run things. I don't want you to be a liberal. But I'm talking about the underlying principle. Democracy means you do your best to look at all the ballots. You try to find the truth."

"Please, Billy. I came over here to talk about us."

"This *is* about us," I said. "We have to agree on the basic stuff. Truth. Fairness. I'm not talking about this damn election anymore. I don't even care who wins. They're both Republicans in my book. I'm talking about what you believe and what I believe."

"Would you listen to yourself?" Darcy said. "This is just politics, Billy. Christ. You're as bad as Gore."

"Don't reduce this to politics. Please. I want us to be able to agree here." I wasn't screaming exactly, but my voice kept throttling up because I could see where we were headed and it made my heart ache.

Darcy shook her head. "I knew this was a mistake. You don't even know what day it is today, do you?" She was speaking softly now, as she did in the sylvan hours, when the ruckus of her life gave way to frank disappointments. This made me want to hold her, to wrap myself along the railing of her hip.

"A year ago, Billy. We met a year ago tonight."

For a moment there it looked as if fairness might prevail. The Florida Supreme Court issued the ruling that should have come down in the beginning: recount the entire state, by hand. But then, of course, the U.S. Supreme Court stepped in to rule that, well, something or other involving equal protection and, more obscurely, the Constitution, and anyway there certainly wasn't enough time to clear this mess up—*such a mess!*—so, you know, don't blame us, we're only trying to help: Bush wins.

All over Washington, Republicans whooped it up. They'd managed to gain the White House and the only cost had been the integrity of every single civil institution in our country. What a bargain! I spent the evening swilling Jack and gingers, howling into Darcy's various machines, imagining I could taste her. Our situation was unclear. By which I mean: she was no longer returning my calls. At around one in the morning I drove to her apartment.

"Go away," she said, through the intercom. "You're drunk."

"I'm not drunk. I love you, honey. I wanna say sorry."

"I'm not going to talk with you, Billy."

"I don't wanna talk about that. I promise. Buzz me in, honey. *Please.*"

She was wearing an old nightgown, the cotton soft and pilled. Her face was a little puffy. Now it was my turn to fall against her, to kiss her brow and plead. Her body stiffened.

"I was wrong," I said. "I was a jerk. Nobody makes me feel like you. We fit, you know. Our bodies, we just fit."

She rose onto the balls of her feet. But she didn't push me away. "You're too angry," she said. "I don't like it when you get so angry."

I sank to my knees and hugged her waist. "I'm sorry. Something takes over. I start thinking too much."

It is true that Darcy was a Republican. But she was still a woman, and as such susceptible to forgiveness. I pressed my cheek against her and breathed warm air into her belly. Her muscles slowly softened.

"No more thinking, Billy. No more arguing. It's over now." With just her fingertips, she hoisted the hem of her nightgown. The tiny blond hairs at the top of her thighs stood on end. My tongue took up the taste of laundry soap. A thick pink scent came from the hollow below.

Could I have known, as she climbed onto the bed and opened herself to me, as I kissed that softest skin, that my anger would rise once again? But who can know these things? They are products of the past, of history finding an apt disguise in the moment. I wanted only to give my beloved this pleasure, to be forgiven. Why, then, as her knees fell open, as her breath bottomed into rasps and her flesh began to pulse, could I think only of James Baker? He rose from the darkest region of my love, his tongue twisted like an old piece of steak. Loathing shimmered around him like an aura. Why was I thinking of this man while Darcy lay open before me like a blossom?

Perhaps because (it occurred to me darkly) Darcy did not view Baker as a bad man at all. She had described him as a righteous man, not unlike her grandpa Tuck. And now suddenly I imagined James

Baker in the humble suit of a country preacher, presiding over my very own wedding.

Darcy was digging her fingers into the meat of my neck, murmuring *go go go.* Her body clenched. This was the life she wanted: a walloping orgasm and the sort of man who knew when to keep his mouth shut. I thought of my own parents, marching into the grim precincts of New Haven to register voters. They had done this. They had believed. My lips felt numb. I wasn't entirely sure I could breathe. Up above, the shuddering began. Darcy's thighs came together in a swirl. How I had loved this moment! The roar of the engines on the runway, the sudden flight. I closed my eyes and breathed in her body. But there was Baker again—and now he was winking at me.

I lifted my head.

Darcy's hands pawed the air. Her mouth puffed my name.

"The Supreme Court," I said, "has filed an emergency injunction."

"No, Billy. *Go.* I'm close." Darcy's eyes were pinched. Her hands had slipped to her breasts, which she gently cupped. Her hip bones stood out like tiny knobs. What in God's name was wrong with me?

"Billy. Come on. Not funny."

I could feel my throat knotting up with sorrow.

Darcy lifted her head from the pillows. Her eyes were starting to clear. "What exactly are you doing here?"

"Once the High Court rules, there are no more appeals."

Darcy drew back. "Do you have any idea how despicably you're behaving? Oh Billy, you really are a sad case." Darcy closed her legs and pulled a sheet across her chest, like a starlet. "The election is over. Don't you get it? *Over.*"

"That's not the issue," I said quietly.

"The issue?" Darcy's fists curled around the sheet. "Do you even know what the issue is anymore? The issue is us, okay? The issue is do you really love me. That's the issue, Billy."

Darcy waited for me to say something heroic. This seemed the thing to do, certainly, to renounce my stingy polemical heart, to affirm the primacy of love. What kind of liberal was I, anyway? And this is surely how it would have gone in the movies, where everything gets absolved in time for the credits. Though I loved Darcy, thrilled to the music of her body, stood in awe of her drive, I could not fathom how I was supposed to live with my disappointment in her.

Nor did I understand, exactly, how she could love me when she found my core beliefs naive and pitiable. Perhaps this was a uniquely Republican gift, the ability to ignore inconvenient contradictions. Or perhaps she was simply better at loving someone without judgment. All that matters is that I failed in that moment to tell her that I loved her.

"You should leave," Darcy said quietly. Her voice floated down in the dark. "Get out of here, Billy. Don't come back."

My friends told me I'd made the right decision. They were extremely reasonable and full of shit. I knew the truth, which was that Darcy was the most exciting lover I would ever take, because I always hated her a little, and never quite understood her, and because she forgave me this and loved me therefore more daringly, without relying on the congruence of our beliefs, the dull compliances of companionship.

I watched the inauguration simply to catch a glimpse of her. She was in the crowd beneath the podium. The camera caught her twice, a pretty woman with ruddy cheeks and a wide sad smile, gazing into the frozen rain.

Soon, she would rise to the office appointed by her talents and give her passion to another man. Eventually, she would move out to Bethesda or Arlington, where the stately oaks and pastures of blue grass survive. She would attach herself to the tasks of motherhood and governance with brilliant loyalty. And she would grow more achingly beautiful by the year, as our regrets inevitably do.

Washington was her town now. I understood that much. I lacked the guile, the gift for compromise, the ability to separate my wishes about the world from the cold facts of the place. I sat on my couch as the oaths were sworn and watched for Darcy's yellow hair, which flickered in the wind that swept across the capitol and then was gone.

Pornography

When I was nineteen I saw two women fistfight on the street in Athens, Greece. The first thing I saw was the big one reach out and smack the little one across the face. She was hideous, the big one. Her face looked like a rusty shovel.

The little one, pretty and blond and slender, shrieked and tried to run. But the big one caught her by the blouse and jerked her back like a fish. The blond turned and swung ineptly, *swung,* as we used to like to say on the playground, *like a girl,* and the big one hit her, a blow which made her nose bleed. The big one smiled and cocked her arm and the blond, appearing to weep blood, shook her head and raised one arm and the big one hit her again and all of us, the men inside the cafe and on the sidewalk, turned from our backgammon boards and dishes of pasty chicken. We heard that damp solid sound and saw the blond fall in a heap and the big one bent to strike again.

But panic evinced some essential guile in the blond. She yanked her tormentor's hair with a fury that seemed momentous and musical. The big one shrieked. Her great ungainly head went down first, followed by her body and her thick voice. The blond climbed to her feet. We assumed now that she would turn and run. But we had underestimated her. She was determined to exact revenge, not just of the hair-pulling variety but with sudden sharp kicks to the face, an effort to harp blood from the place where blood is most easily had.

Can I tell you there was something delicate in it all? Or that we men saw nothing of our own role? Or stepped in to put an end to the violence? No. Only that no one laughed, not the drunks pleading the doorways for sleep, nor the shop merchants clenching drachmae, nor the toothless backgammon king whose hand cupped the dice abstemiously. (And certainly not me. I merely stood trying to make sense of the damp buzz in my knuckles, the clench around my groin.)

The blond was wearing high-heeled boots. This seemed an absurd thing to wear in the midst of a street fight. But she was a beautiful girl, after all. She was not, presumably, a street fighter by trade. She kicked gracefully, but her balance was poor and the big one soon toppled her and clamped on to her, their movements close and ardent, and this intimacy we watched too, drawn to the hot puffs of air, the raked skin and grime taken up from the pavement.

A young policeman happened by and set his hand gently on the butt of his club. It pained him, I think, to imagine taking some significant role in the drama. But then the man at the center of it appeared suddenly, a meager man it must be said, with an oily toupee and cheap vinyl shoes, chopping his hands like a conductor, shouting uselessly and turning to us. He bent down and attempted to pry the big woman loose. He took hold under her arms and whispered in her ear. After a minute or so she released her grip and allowed herself to be borne up. In a gesture of chivalry abjectly unsuited to the moment, the man threw his coat over her tattered dress and hustled her from the scene.

There lay the blond after all this, her shirt torn off, her face a hideously tender swirl. The young policeman, rising to his duty reluctantly, helped her to her feet and led her slowly away, while we men in the crowd took in the flagrant unintended sway of her body, her pale lovely breasts streaked in blood, her legs showing nasty welts. We watched her in silence, watched her for as long as we could see her, sorely disappointed in ourselves, savoring this disappointment, waiting as shame forever waits to feel desire again.

The Body
in Extremis

I had just moved from a small city to a big one. The small city had been no good for me. I found myself getting into extreme and ridiculous conflicts. The woman who considered me her protégé called me up drunk one night, hungry for flirtation, and grew furious when I didn't reciprocate. I nearly came to blows with my landlord. People reacted to me somewhat too strongly. Frequently they would ask: "Are you from New York?"

The big city was better. The people dressed sharper and spoke quickly. They had a sense of distraction, which kept bullshit to a minimum. The theaters got all the movies. The buskers didn't suck.

The night I left the small city, my friend Pam told me to look up her friend who had just moved to the big city. She showed me a photo, a half-profile shot, and from this photo I could see that Ling was Chinese and that she had nice legs. She was leaning back in a chair, smoking a cigarette. She looked to be assuming a posture of cool.

I thought: *I would like to fuck her.*

Whenever I see a photo of a desirable woman, even a reasonably desirable woman, even a woman not so especially desirable but in possession of one desirable quality, I think about fucking her. Sometimes I don't even need a photo. Sometimes just a description, or a name, and I start to think: *Yes, Monique, what would it be like with Monique?* I think about fucking Jane Pauley. I think about fucking Princess Diana (or did). I thought once, briefly, about fucking Julia Child. Most men run women through this imaginative combine. If they are honest, they admit to these impulses. And if they are decent, they do not act on them.

My fantasies are rarely specific. Please don't get that idea. I don't see laced limbs or trembly snatch. I envision a more general sense. Could I convince her to have me? Run my fingers over her palest skin? What is she like naked? What sounds would she make? Like that. What would this be like, the intimacy, the security? Probably it has something to do with possession.

I'd come for the job, which involved teaching composition to eighteen-year-olds. I was thirty-four then. My friends were all married. Most had kids. I would call them on weekends and listen to the happy chaos in the background. I was a godfather three times.

I had started to pay inordinate attention to my hairline. There was some careful combing going on. Not a combover. Nothing that sad or drastic. But some combing down, to obscure a creeping widow's peak. I would thumb through the fancy magazines and stare at the ads for stomach flatteners and heed their grave warnings about *gut displacement*. I knew this concept to exist. It had been some time since I was able to button my trousers without discomfort.

I did not do much socializing. This is one of my weaknesses. I have always been maladaptive when it comes to moving, though, oddly, I have moved eleven times since college. I'm not exactly sure

how one meets people, if not through work. Bars and personal ads—
no. These call for a marriage of bravado and innocence I can never
swing.

About two weeks in, I called Ling. She had a deep voice, kind
of mannish, which I hadn't expected. She spoke quickly, with an air
of nonchalance. She used various kinds of slang. She told me she
was from San Francisco, but when I pressed the point she admitted
that she had left there at six. She had grown up in Southern California—*bingo*, I thought—though she understood this to be a point of
indictment, mitigated by the fact that she had gone to college and
worked, briefly, in northern California. She was twenty-two years
old.

Ling's apartment was at the end of a small alley, on the top floor of
an old house. The place smelled of wet carpet and rotting wood. It
was cozy. Low ceiling, futon couch, CDs in a milk crate, some fancy
new appliances her mother had bought for her. Her features were
broad and sort of gummy. Her nose looked like a lump of clay that
had been flattened by someone's thumb. Her ass, though, was im-
pressively shelfed, not a trace of that flat Asian business. She wore
thin corduroy pants and a top that made visible a band of skin along
her lower back.

On the way to the movie we passed a young couple studded
with piercings.

"I know a girl with vertical bars through her nipples," Ling
said.

"Bars?"

"They increase the sensation."

"Wouldn't you worry about them ripping?"

"I wouldn't," Ling said. "No."

Ling was a grad student in mechanical engineering. She seemed determined not to let this dampen her self-image, which was that of a reprobate hipster. She was sexually frank. She smoked. She drank and talked excessively of drinking. She listened to bands with names like Pavement and Loaf, whose appeal was predicated on a desire not to express much effort. Behind this posed sangfroid, of course, was the inner panic nurtured by ambitious immigrant families. But Ling, an early grade skipper, learned how to get along among her elders— the necessary tamping of neurotic impulses. She was a hard worker who liked to appear careless. She worked hard at appearing careless.

My essential problem, a symptom, anyway, of my essential problem at that time, was that I had grown to crave sex, the release and congress, the awkward pungent business of bodies in extremis. Sexual ideation dominated my thoughts. I masturbated up to four times a day, and did so mainly to eliminate the distraction, so I could get my work done.

What I wanted was a body, a female body, lifted off its feet and set down again, an entirely new back and chest and ass and ribs. But I was uniquely unqualified to find one. I spent my days lecturing toothsome and pimpled teenagers and my evenings alone, grading papers, taking on the editing necessary to make adjunct work sustainable. And masturbating.

There were no sparks or colors when I hung out with Ling, not even the trill of an exercised pulse. There were, instead, indications. Indications of a possible arrangement.

✷ ✷ ✷

"Beyond Seven," Ling said. "Those are the best."

"Never heard of them," I said.

"They're the best," she said.

"How do you know?"

"How do you think?"

"That makes a difference, does it?"

Ling laughed in a way suggesting my pitiful ignorance. Not for the first time in dealing with her, I felt the gap in our ages. She had grown up in late Reagan America and come of age sexually at the height of the AIDS epidemic. To her, the protocol of condoms was second nature, assumed. I still viewed them as somehow illicit.

"Of course it does. It's inside you, David. It's right up against you."

Ling took a drag on her cigarette. She was a vegetarian on moral grounds but smoked Camel Lights, because they had the most taste. Her lips were fat but nicely shaped. They sat on her face like rain-puffed blossoms.

There was the night of the Scrabble and of the Jack Daniels, which she brought over to my place. We had exchanged emails regarding drinking rules. Any word over 50 points earned a shot, a seven-letter word meant two shots, and so on. These were unnecessary. We were both eager to drink and be drunk and then she was on the floor with her back turned, looking at one of my CDs, that band of perfectly hairless skin visible. My hands moved to her shoulders.

There is that moment of suspense—will the pass be turned away?—and then, once that is over, there is the delicious question of how undressing will proceed. It was she who let out a little noise, a guttural sound, and said, "Let's go lie down."

From the beginning our sexual coupling was marked by a ferocious intensity and endurance. That first night we screwed for an hour, stopped, started again. This went on until morning. We moved with such ardor that we had to pause to catch our breath. First with her on top, sliding down and nodding quickly as I clutched the meat of her hips. Then flipping, her knees holstering my hips, and a long testing of angles, velocities. She hoisted her legs up and flopped on her belly. In the course of all this tangling, we stumbled on to a position in which we scissored our legs, our pelvises swung into unhindered union. We were both stunned and, afterwards, lay together trying to make sense of this force, thinking and sometimes saying things like *woof* and *dang*. Giggling.

I am not speaking here of any unusual prowess. It was only a stunning alignment of nerve endings and needs. I had met someone, at last, as purely greedy for sensation, as gluttonous for attainable pleasure. *Woof.*

On Thanksgiving our friend Pam visited, with some other friends. Ling advised that we say nothing about our arrangement. There was no reason, she said. We both knew what this was. Telling Pam would only complicate things. I agreed. "It's not like we make each other weak in the knees," she said, and I ignored the edge of contempt in her tone.

Oh, we thought we were such sly dogs, teasing each other with gropes and lecherous gestures, acting out a formality that amused us, made us feel empowered by our naughty secret. When all the guests cleared out, we tore at one another. Afterward, naked and tingling and briny-smelling, we pretended that Pam stood in the doorway.

"It slipped in," I said and Ling said "a few hundred times" and I said "it just slipped—you know how things slip?" and Ling said "it kept slipping harder and harder" and I said "you didn't tell me Ling was such a wet girl" and she said, "you should have mentioned David's condition" and I said, "do all your friends suck like that?" and she said "it's all I can do to get him to soften up for a minute" and I said "are all your friends so multiply orgasmic?" and she said "slippage, major-league slippage" and I began to hum "Slip Slidin' Away."

As I moved into her, Ling would suck at one of my lips. She told me she felt the urge to bite. She liked rough behavior, liked me to grab her breasts and squeeze hard enough to leave bruises. Her nipples budded out from a chest that was nearly flat. They were keenly sensitive, and slightly larger at the tip than the base, like Frankenstein's bolts. She enjoyed having them bitten at. She liked for me to slam into her at unpredicted intervals, liked the aggression, the jolt, maybe even the sense of violation, and sometimes braced her hands against the wall above her head. She wanted to be rubbed, every place and hard. Anything was just fine, really, though she favored positions that allowed her mouth to suck and bite at mine.

The face becomes new in sex. A face like Ling's, which was flat, a bit bland, takes on a wondrous animation. The Asian face appears less expressive to Caucasians because it has fewer angles and hollows and shadows. Less drama. But, of course, it is no less expressive.

Ling's cheeks were plump and squarish. Her large jaw operated at a slight underbite, which made her look fish-mouthed. Her
eyes were set shallow, and half hidden by folds of skin. Her eyebrows were rectangular and poorly defined. Even her ears were ungainly; they looked chewed on and oversized—the ears of an old
man mistakenly latched onto a young woman's skull.

But the transformation of this face: Her eyes widened and
blurred. The tiny patch of skin between her eyebrows knit. Her lips
pooched seductively. Blood worked to the surface of her clammy
skin and crept up her neck and across her cheeks in red swaths.
Sometimes, I would catch sight of her nose, from below, and mar-
vel at the perfect roundness of her nostrils. The entirety of her face
conveyed tremendous concentration, a determined labor toward
surrender. In these moments, everything blunt and indelicate became
preciously unhinged. She looked like a very young girl, overcome
by the capabilities of her body, simultaneously thrilled and terrified, her wide mouth made panicky. I could not listen to her noises
without losing control of my heartbeat, just as I cannot think of them
at this moment without growing hard and lonesome.

Ling's entire physique suggested a dichotomy, a dull beauty
and its more alluring underside. Her hair was thick and long and
coarse in the way of Asians. It hung wild and helped feminize her,
certainly, and was a terrific sexual prop, though it fell out in clumps,
and caused little bald spots about which she was disturbingly frank.

She was clumsy. Her waist was slung low and poorly defined;
her belly sprawled. Her arms were thick and muscled, her shoulders
as broad as my own. But you had only to witness the way she fo-
cused this power, torquing furiously, rising and falling, nimble and
newly taut, to understand that her body found an almost perfect

grace in bed. Her sex, too, was lovely, hidden deep in an intricate, pink-purple pattern that reminded me of the way cream introduces itself to coffee.

It was the imperfections that captured me, finally, because these required some special effort at tolerance, which, after a time, matured into an unexpected and indelible affection. Her pubic hair: patchy, tufted, an undoing of the loveliness below. Her feet: flat and rough, like thin spades. Her fingernails: ragged, bitten, like mine, to the nubs.

Ling called herself "a big aggressive Asian girl" and boasted to me that she could never find clothing that fit when she went to visit her family in China. She burped and cracked her knuckles. She enjoyed getting blotto to the point where she could act on her sloppier impulses. A week after we'd first slept together she called me at one in the morning, from a bar. "Hey," she said. "Hey."

I had been sleeping.

"I'm not going home alone," she said. "Are you going to pick me up?"

And yet, when she was safely in my apartment, the frat-boy swagger dissolved into a hopeful sway. She wanted her lover man, her new lover man, and she wanted her clothes off and tugged at them without much success and when I led her into the bedroom she was shy and grateful.

That night, as on others, there came a moment when we looked at one another, our swollen fulsome bodies, and tried to figure out how it could feel so good and right and natural in this one uncontainable way. We knew we were engaged in an arrangement, that expedience hung around the proceedings. But with our bodies there, negotiating for us, our flags of skin unfurled, a certain holiness took hold, and we had to look away from one another's faces, and sink our teeth into the cream of necks and shoulders.

What I mean to say is that beneath all the orgasmic pyrotechnics, the calibrated hedonism, there was a tenderness. Sometimes, after we were finished, I would lie atop her, my body incoherent with bliss. In time, her breath grew labored, and I would tense, knowing I was crushing her, and she would lace her arms around me and murmur *not quite yet* and we would lie there yet a while, touching as much of each other as we could.

But then, always, there was the life beyond the mattress, and the long, uncertain evenings waiting, like children trapped at the grown-up table, till we could be excused to the pursuit of one another's bodies. We suffered the regular disappointment of facing each other, across some restaurant table, with little to say.

Because of her youth, she relied on a repertoire of stories from her college days, all of which she prefaced with the phrase "Oh, this was so hilarious" and none of which were in fact hilarious, but closer to mundane, often tragically so. (I listened to the story of how she mispronounced the word *erogenous* during college orientation—she emphasized the third syllable, erog*en*ous—at least four times.)

My own whinging could not have been any less annoying. I was, perhaps, a bit more polished. I didn't repeat my stories. But the themes were always the same: neurotic screeds against nincompoop supervisors and dim-witted students.

We played at interest, made the necessary talk, joked when we could. In this way we contrived to justify what would happen later.

*   *   *

In the sack, we outfoxed artifice; our charms and commonalities snuck out. Ling discussed her family, revealing a ridiculous wealth she kept assiduously hidden, the secret decadence of private cooks and exotic fruits, a deep dynastic loyalty. When she spoke Chinese, her mouth widened and her pitch leaped and her tongue moved over the words in butterfly motions.

I read to her in a soft voice and spooned her long body and warmed the caps of her tush with my newly plump belly. Sometimes she set her old man's ears against my fuzzy chest and listened to me warble like old Bob Dylan until she fell asleep. In the morning, I prepared elaborate breakfasts and brought her tea and honey, and after we had eaten, still naked, our appetites revved, we spent the morning writhing, able to see everything and freshening the bed with new commotions.

But then there would be the drive back to her apartment, during which we would find ourselves sadly reawakened to how little regard we held for one another. She was, again, a trendy, groping young woman. And I, again, an aging pedagogue with a blue streak a mile wide.

Around Christmas Ling had made an abrupt decision: we needed to set a timetable to stop sleeping together. I agreed, not because I agreed but because agreement was required to keep the Good Ship Libido seaworthy. Had I pushed then, had I questioned why limits needed to be set at all, I felt sure Ling would have pulled anchor. The date set for the kiss-off was February 14. I had suggested it, in a moment of mordant whimsy, and Ling ratified immediately. That gave us a month, upon her return from winter break.

* * *

If absence makes the heart grow fonder, ultimatum makes the heart grow feral. In bed, Ling ordered me to hold her arms down, like a captive, and I moved into her so hard I could feel the tendons in my groin strain against her pelvic bone, and sometimes heard, or imagined I heard, an ominous and thrilling snap. And when she lowered herself onto me, she ordered me to smack her lovely behind with increasing vigor, until the sound echoed off the wood beams above my bed and I felt her begin pulsing involuntarily.

The notion of safe sex—a notion she held to reflexively on paper—flew out the window. We licked one another everywhere and transferred with our frantic tongues the sweat and spit and other darkly guarded smells that mix on the sheets and come to stand for sex in our scent memory. Had we looked at this behavior in a sober light . . . but, you see, that's not where we were. We were in the other place. For the ten or twelve or fourteen hours in my cavelike bedroom, the only rule was gratification. Sleep was kept to a minimum, not by choice but by the exuberance of our bodies, which could not keep still or apart.

On Valentine's Day, a Friday, we climbed into bed and did not emerge until the next evening. Ling had her period, her flow unusually heavy. Long after I had driven her home I stood in front of my bathroom mirror and admired the dried blood on my midriff and smelled its sweet metal stink and picked at the clots, quietly adoring the image of a passion that left these marks and later lowering myself into a hot bath, where the water stained an excellent crimson before fading.

* * *

It is never over, and especially when the body has clear motive. We lasted ten days, two weeks, stiff in our new rules, and, when punished sufficiently, we surrendered in a plunge, closer to our loss and ashamed and more voracious than ever.

Or, I should say, Ling seemed more ashamed.

My take on the situation was more forgiving. When you have lived a longer time in your body, and suffered more the loneliness of disuse, gratitude comes cheaper. As I told her, I was only too glad to continue our arrangement, though she seemed nonplussed by this ease. The important thing, we agreed, was that we part ways gracefully, because we had this dear mutual friend, Pam, who was now considering moving to our city. And so we held fast to the bleary notion that what we did to one another sexually could be segued into a low-voltage friendship. If we were careful, considerate.

I was not terribly concerned about Ling. She had a heart from the new school. That is how I understood things to be. I was more concerned at my own behavior, the way rejected longing might cause me to lash out and spoil everything. I did not consider the extent of her feelings. I did not consider the way she occasionally pushed my name into the dark between us—*David, David*—her voice a wet reed, her eyes turned away, as if to hide or disown.

Men store their own private stock of memories, those visual haunts that remind us, in times of yearning. With a torturing clarity, I can see one old girlfriend, seating and unseating herself on my lap, her bottom blue in the moonlight, roundly swallowing. Another, arching her back, lacing her calves around mine, and gushing. Or Ling, pooled beneath me, having already been worked to the end and back, dragging her fingers down her nose and lips, asking me to come, *right here.*

Was this degradation, or do the extremes of passion allow for a more supple view? I can say only that I wanted nothing more than this prompt, the chance to stain her, to display what she elicited, to stripe her from cheek to belly. This pleased us, this joyous dirtiness, and we finger-painted her torso, until, with a towel I fetched, she wiped me off.

We were on the way to the airport to pick up Pam when Ling turned to me and said: "I'm seeing someone new." My heart began a halftime faster. I suffered the inward panic of a man whose good fortune has run out. I stared at the black, rain-slicked highway, at the downtown buildings gilded in light. Quickly, to stanch my confusion, I said, "That's great. I think that's great."

Ling added—in that deep voice of hers, flat as a frozen pond— "I mean, we both know where we are."

"Right," I said.

She asked if I might not want to hear a little about the fellow. It was a cruel question, all things considered, but we were playing roles now. That is where we had come to. We were friends now. And friends listened to friends moon over new lovers.

He was a classmate of hers, a fellow engineer. He had built a robotic fish that much impressed her. I had listened to her rave about this fish before, and had wondered out loud as to its purpose. Was it intended for research? Was there some practical application? Did the world especially need a robotic fish? Might a robotic fisherman, all things considered, be a better investment of know-how? That wasn't the point, Ling had told me. I was missing the point.

That she had decided to end our arrangement on the way to the airport to pick up our mutual friend, dropping it into conversation as an afterthought—this was an act of provocation. Yes. But she was twenty-two years old, in over her head, and no doubt terrified of my reaction. It was inconsiderate. Yet, from an engineering standpoint, sound methodology. She had chosen a time that would ensure minimum recoil.

And so, the business of the airport pick up. Ling stomped along in her ridiculous army boots, telling her stupid stories, while I stumbled about in a red silence. Inside the terminal, I found a bathroom and stared at myself in the mirror, my stupid, combed-forward hair. The guy at the sink next to me said, "You lose your luggage, too?"

When I emerged Pam was there, bright, friendly Pam, who knew nothing of the situation, thought, instead, that she was visiting two pals, who, to her delight, enjoyed a casual friendship. She and Ling spent the trip home gabbing boisterously while I pretended to concentrate on the wet roads.

The next evening Pam and I went to pick up Ling for dinner. We clomped up the stairs to her place. I'd had cocktails in preparation. The lights were on inside but the door was locked. We knocked and shouted, knocked again. A minute or so passed. There was maybe some vague scramble and murmur, and I suppose I had an inkling, somewhere, though I was trusting enough, or vain enough, or fragile enough, to hide this from myself. We figured Ling was in the shower.

Pam pulled out her key and slipped it into the lock and opened the door and before us stood a young man, disheveled and blushing. From the corner of my eye I saw the bathroom door quickly shut. It was, for that long moment, like the revelations delivered in dreams: astonishing yet inevitable. *How could she?* and *Of course.* It wasn't what I saw that was so difficult to bear, but, like the hacks buzzing away on TV always say, it was the cover-up, the way in which they hadn't been undressed and groping, drunk on one another's mouths, struggling into clothing.

"You must be John," Pam said. "I've heard all about *you.*" She ushered him to a seat at Ling's small kitchen table. "What have you two been up to? Studying? A little study group?" She laughed. "We're going to dinner, John. Come with us."

Flushed with sheepish pleasure, as lost to the real action as Pam, John tried to frown. "I've got homework to do."

Homework, I thought. *Christ.*

"You can do that later," Pam said. "You've got all night."

I sat down across from John, the Fishboy, studying his face, as if for some indication of why he would make Ling's knees weak. He had a thick mouth, sleepy eyes, a tangled hedge of brown hair. He was young, as she was. And I was an old man made silly by my affections.

"We'll only be about an hour," I said helpfully.

Fishboy tried again to frown.

"Of course you'll come," Pam said.

And now Ling emerged from the bathroom and strode over to Pam and gave her a little hug, and smiled with embarrassed glee. Pam went to take a pee and Ling sat herself at the head of the table, with Fishboy on one side and me on the other.

I thought about Ling's mouth, wide, fishy, the happy industry of her motions, sweeping her black hair away, her tongue extending, the two surfaces meeting, the intimacy with which she outlined my shape, how hungry she had been and how I needed that hunger and how that mouth would now be fixed on this new body and had been in the moments when Pam and I were rising up the stairs.

"What sort of homework do you have to do?" I asked Fishboy.

He held up a textbook. "Design stuff. Same as Ling."

"Cool."

"And you're a teacher, right?" he said. "Ling told me about you."

I nodded and fiddled with my key ring. I wanted terribly not to let my feelings show. And, at the same time, I wanted to punch Ling in the face. I wanted to shake her so hard her skull would buckle against the wall.

Pam emerged from the bathroom and some minutes were spent discussing where we might dine. Pam continued to urge Fishboy to come along. I did, as well. What a good sport I was! What a jolly good fellow! He finally begged off. Ling said, "I'll walk you out" and stumbled after him. They spent a minute in the hallway, groping.

"Were we early?" I asked Pam.

She laughed. "Apparently."

There is a point at which self-preservation demands pride, no matter how hollow. Ling pretends she has done nothing wrong, and I pretend I am not reeling. This was our dinner, Pam gabbing along idiotically. I looked at Ling only once. A flush of red skin snaked from her neck to the center of her cheek. Sex rash. I was certain if I looked again I would begin to shake.

When you are betrayed to this extent, and in this way, a kind of dissonance prevails. There is the person you knew before, and there is the person you know now. And they are not the same person. So that, when you think about them, it is only as a way of understanding what you have lost, what you will never have again. You become wed to the dross of memory, a person who lies alone in bed and thinks about what has already happened.

We had wanted to end things neatly. That is what we had both vowed, right? But the way things had gone, the way Ling had jury-rigged them, seemed devised to ensure the opposite. My initial sense was that she had felt pressured by me, or frightened, had sensed the bruising loneliness of my life, the way in which I clutched at the world around me, and opted to expulse me from her life in such a manner that no clinging would ensue.

My friends insisted she was terribly angry at me for the way in which I had ravaged her body and dismissed the rest of her. Perhaps she had been more shamed by our relationship than I'd realized, the way it sought a convenient path from isolation. And perhaps, once she had found her own way, I came to represent a desperate past. But then there was the matter of our sexual relationship. And nothing there had ever been fake, or dull, or shameful. If anything, the sensations there had been too real, out of proportion. Perhaps these scared her. Perhaps, as a young woman of twenty-two, she had felt that the only way to exorcise this sexual possession was to stage a public renunciation.

It doesn't much matter. Most of these feelings were subconscious, nothing she would admit. She would say, only, that she had lost track of time, had made a mistake, but not a terribly large one, because, after all, she had announced an end to our agreement. In the strict terms favored by lawyers, or engineers, she had done nothing wrong.

This discernment of motive did nothing, anyhow, to undo or diminish my pain. It was just something I thought about so I did not have to think about the coming blue, waiting there with its rolling pin, or what Ling—or any of the Lings of this wide world— might be doing, at that late hour, in her cozy apartment across our big city.

When you have spent as long inside yourself as I have you learn a certain humility in the face of hardship. And then you learn it again. It takes years to become as softhearted and hopeful as I am. I had no business dancing with a young woman like that. I should have known better.

The heart is not only a lonely hunter, though it is certainly that. It is a drowning salesman, a bloodied clown, an incurable disease. We pay dearly for its every decision. There are a lucky few, dead in certain vital places, who learn to tame their passions.

But I am certain that you, too, have some episode in your life that lines up against this one, some mad period of transgression in which your body, your foolish foolish body, led you toward tender ruin. And sometimes, at night, you must lie awake and ask yourself: How could I have done this? How ever, in the world, might I have become such a fool? How do I stop? And when? When? When will I have her again?

Acknowledgments

This book would not exist but for the grace of the following kickass human beings: Richard and Barbara Almond, Peter Almond, Alice Rosenthal, Tom Finkel, Pablo Salopek, Holden Lewis, Pat Flood, Emma Trelles, Ann Clark Espuelas, Keith Morris, Victor Cruz, Liz Vondrak, Rachel Garber, Kirk Semple, Amy Williams, Dave Blair, Jim Clark, Tim Huggins, Ana Jamolca, Jenni Price, Lad Tobin, Eve Bridburg, Shane Dubow, and Steve Amick. Thanks to all the editors who have supported my work, in particular Adrienne Brodeur, Alice Turner, Jodee Rubins, Michael Griffith, Colleen Donfield, Lois Hauselman, Michael Czyzniejewski, and, of course, Brendan Cahill. Thanks, finally, to all my wonderful my students, who have taught me as much as I taught them.